GIRLFIEND

by

Jacquelyn Faye

GIRLFIEND

ISBN: 978-1-945893-17-9

First Publication, June 2020

Published by Untold Press LLC
114 NE Estia Lane
Port St Lucie, FL 34983

www.untoldpress.com

PRODUCED IN THE UNITED STATES OF AMERICA

10 9 8 7 6 5 4 3 2 1

DEDICATON

This book is dedicated to all the crazy girlfriends out there.
You keep that shit up.

CHAPTER 1

I tightened the straps on my backpack a little higher while staring at the entrance to Woodrow Wilson High School. It wasn't uncomfortable or bouncing against my back; I was simply stalling for time, finding any possible excuse not to go in. I looked up at the sky to see if there were any stray meteors hurtling toward Earth. *Anything.*

"Please, God."

A car backfired behind me, scaring the shit out of me. My mother drove away in her 1987 Mercury Cougar. I waved, silently pleading for her to change her mind.

She wouldn't. I'd asked her at least two-hundred-and-thirty-seven times last night. I'm surprised she didn't drag me into the school by my ponytail. The one she had threatened to cut off at least two-hundred-and-thirty-*eight* times. She said guys didn't have long hair twice as many times as that. We were very repetitive.

"Move it, douche." A jock shoulder-checked me as he walked past.

I sighed and shook my head. It was starting already.

Forcing my feet to move, I slowly trudged my way into what was sure to be the start of a completely hellish hundred-and-eighty-day nightmare. My senior year.

Not just the final year of my illustrious high school career, either. The first day of my final year at a completely new school in a brand-new town. Technically the town

7

wasn't brand new. I was new. In it. It had been around for a couple of hundred years. As had most of Virginia. But Mom and Dad split up right before summer break, and Mom's new job had relocated us to this shining bastion of America's South. I didn't quite understand how it was considered the South. Sure, it fell south of the Mason-Dixon line, but it was like in the middle of the fricking country.

Half of the people I talked to had a southern drawl. The other half didn't. Whatever. At least it didn't snow as much as it had in Chicago. It was almost September, and I would've been comfortable wearing shorts to school. If they were part of the dress code.

The last few stragglers heading into the school started running for the door. Great. I was going to be late on my first day.

Suck it up, Dane.

I booked it. I was the last one in the door before the endless droning of the electric bell, conveniently located over my head, blared. Even after it stopped, I could hear the metallic echoes in my head.

"You just made it."

I looked up at the giant standing off to the side of the front door. He stood over six-and-a-half feet. His head had been cleanly shaved except for a black flat-top that looked like the landing strip on an aircraft carrier. It didn't look real. His muscular arms were crossed over his chest and the sleeves on his shirt looked like they were one muscle flex away from splitting up the seams. Even the thighs of his freshly pressed gray slacks were straining.

I gulped. "Yeah. First day. I kind of got lost."

He turned his gaze away from the glass entrance and focused his twin ocular orbs on me. I expected a death-ray to vaporize me any moment. "You were standing there for five minutes, son. You just didn't want to come in. Office is to the left if you need to check in." He slowly faced forward, ignoring me further.

I nodded and did as he suggested. I didn't want to get eaten.

The school office was the first glass double door on the left. A line of students stood in front of the counter. I smiled inwardly. It might be lunch time before I got to my first class...

"You're tardy, Miss Fern."

"I'm always tardy, Principal Edwards."

"And always such a joy. Get a tardy slip."

"Wouldn't want to miss my morning chat with the dean..."

I opened the door to the office and let the petite, purple-haired girl in the jeans and black hoodie enter ahead of me. My sole intention had been to buy a few more precious moments before actually starting class.

"'*I'm going to hold the door for the girl, so I can stand behind her and stare at her ass?*' I don't think so. You go first."

I stared at her in complete and utter confusion. "Excuse me?"

She pulled her hands out of her hoodie pockets and held one palm up while making walking gestures with the other. "You walk in office first. Me go second. You no stand behind me and look at butt."

I rolled my eyes and entered, not bothering to hold it for her. I heard her catch it with her foot as I stood right in the doorway, not able to move in farther because of the line.

"Are you going in?"

I looked at her over my shoulder. "If you had bothered to look inside before you accused me of leering, you might have noticed the line. I was being polite and going to stand in the hall and hold the door. There's no room to go in yet."

9

I felt her hand on my arm as she gently pushed me aside and peered into the over-full office.

"Shit. Oh, well. This beats sitting in class." Without letting go of my arm she looked up at me. "Sorry. I'm bitchy until I've had my fifth coffee."

"It's okay."

She cracked her gum, and I could feel her staring at me. "Were you late, too?"

"No. Just transferred. First day."

"Senior?"

I nodded, not really wanting to continue the conversation. She was adorably cute, in an elfin sort of way, but that much attitude wasn't exactly worth the headache.

"You're not very chatty, are you?"

I looked back over my shoulder and sighed. "No."

"What school did you go to last year?"

"Saint Viators."

"Never heard of it."

"Probably because it's in Chicago."

"You just move here?"

"Yes."

"Why?"

I sighed. She went from bitchy to wouldn't-shut-the-hell-up in under a minute. The student at the counter finished, and the line ambled forward, giving Fern enough room to get in and shut the door. Right in the face of the student trying to leave.

"Thanks, Fern." The girl trying to get to class shot her an angry glare.

"Oops. Sorry. I had my bitch radar off."

"Kept detecting yourself?" The blonde practically kicked the door open and slinked through, slipping her paperwork into her bag.

"So why on God's green earth would you move to Oak Hills?"

"I have my lovely mother to thank. She and my dad split up, and we moved here for her work."

"What work?"

"Do you always ask this many questions?"

"I do when I'm bored. I'm bored. And you're new."

"Lucky me. She's a store manager for Good Buy. They offered her a promotion if she came out here."

"Cool. I like Good Buy."

I sighed. "Me, too."

The line shuffled forward one more. I almost *wanted* to get to class. Almost.

"So, I'm Lucy. But everybody calls me Fern."

"Why?"

"It's my last name?"

"Your name is Lucy Fern. *Lucyfern*..."

"Yep. I know. Har har. My mom thought it was hilarious."

"It is. Kinda. I'm Dane. Evans."

She held out her hand. I shook it and almost pulled back from her grip. Every girl in the universe usually had cold hands. Not Lucy. Hers were hot. And to be honest, kind of clammy. I resisted the urge to wipe my palm on my jeans, settling for sticking it in my pocket.

"So, do you know what classes you're in yet?"

"No. I'm picking up my schedule."

"You could have downloaded it last week..."

"We were moving and don't even have the house set up yet. My computer is still on the moving truck."

"Ahh. Too bad. You could have saved yourself an hour this morning."

"Not in a rush."

"You don't like school?"

"No, I just don't like people."

"But you like me."

I shot her another glance over my shoulder.

"Come on, admit it. You like me. I'm charming and cute."

I refused to take the bait.

"Dane likes Fern. Dane likes Fern," she started chanting in the office.

I spun around and resisted covering her mouth with my hand.

She flashed me a wicked grin. "See. Told you."

I sighed. "Fern. Look. I'm sure you're a very nice person. Deep down. Abysmally deep. Somewhere near your core. But I don't like to stand out. At all. So, if you could keep it down, I would *really* appreciate it."

"Nerp."

"Nerp? What the hell is a nerp?"

"That means no."

"Nerp means no?"

"Yerp."

I wanted to scream in frustration. I'd pictured my first day going horribly wrong in so, so many different ways. Being tortured by a purple-haired pixie in a hoodie *wasn't* one of them. "Fern. Are you on any drugs I, as your fellow classmate, should be made aware of in case you overdose?"

"*Nein.*"

"Nine of them?"

"Nerp. *Nein* means no in German."

"You speak German?"

"*Non.*"

"Was that French?"

"*Oui...*"

"You speak French but not German?"

"*Nein.* But I learned how to say no in twenty-seven languages."

"Um. Okay. Why twenty-seven?"

"Three cubed. I've always *adored* that number for some reason. Three times three times three."

I kind of wanted to motion for security. Fern was nuttier than a fruit loop. "Okay then."

"Just think. If you hadn't wanted to stare at my butt, we wouldn't have been able to have this conversation."

"Yeah."

"See. Told you that you wanted to see my butt."

"What? No. What the hell, Fern?"

Everybody in the office turned around, and I held up my hands protesting my innocence. The red-haired, severe woman standing behind the counter gave me a disgusted look.

The glass door behind us opened, and Principal Edwards walked into the office. He spotted the line and Fern standing behind me. "Come on back, Fern. I'll let Dean Winchester know you're waiting to see him."

"Joy. I'll see you at lunch, Dane?"

"Not if I hide hard enough. Have fun, Fern."

She shot me an evil grin, wiggled her eyebrows, and followed Edwards into the bowels of the school office. For the first time since I'd left Chicago, I let out a sigh of relief and relaxed. Until I saw everyone *still* staring at me. I just shook my head and pointed in the direction Fern had gone.

More than a few of them nodded in understanding.

CHAPTER 2

I'd made it in time for English Lit. According to my schedule, I missed Marine Biology. Disappointing. I was hoping to miss Trig, but that was one of my last classes. I could see the teacher through the square of glass in the door, standing at her desk and talking to the class instead of behind the podium. I knocked softly on the thick wooden door.

The teacher stopped talking and looked through the window. Seeing me standing there, she waved me in.

"Hi. I'm Dane. Sorry, I'm late. I just got my schedule."

"The transfer student, right?"

"Yes, ma'am."

She grabbed the seating chart off her desk and quickly scanned through it, finding my name. "Yep. You're on here. You get a window seat in the back." She pointed to one of the empty desks in the rear of the class. Right next to a very familiar purple head. I sighed and awkwardly walked across the room and down the aisle to my seat.

"Hi, Daaaaane," she said sweetly as I sat next to her, dumping my backpack next to me.

"Hi, Fern."

"This is a coincidence, isn't it?"

"No. Pretty sure God hates me."

"Pretty sure he hates all the humans. You're such a disappointment."

I shook my head, not remotely wanting to have a religious discussion with her. I was afraid of what she might worship in her basement. The longer I spent in her presence, the more I was sure chickens or goats might be involved...

I reached into my backpack and pulled out the new English Lit book I had gotten at the office.

"Now, as I was saying, I want you to take your syllabus home, really go through it. It basically tells you everything you will need to know to pass my class. This is English Lit. You won't be able to bluff your way through it. You're going to have to read the assignments. Some of them are pretty difficult. If you have any trouble...Google it. You guys are lucky. We didn't have that when I was your age. There is *no* reason *not* to pass. You have all the knowledge of the world literally at your fingertips. If you fail my tests, quizzes, or homework, I'll assume you don't care about my class and my opinion of you will fall below that of a single cell organism. No excuses. Consider that my motto. Does everyone understand? Fern? I'm talking to you, too."

"Yes, Miss Jacoby. Use the internets."

"Yes, Fern. And let's try to do our homework this year?"

"Yes, Miss Jacoby."

The teacher rolled her eyes when Fern's eyes never left the ceiling tiles above her. Then she droned on about the syllabus, line by line.

"You had this class?" I whispered.

"No. She teaches World Lit, too. Had that last year." She lowered her eyes and looked over at me, giving me a little smile. "I like your hair."

"Thanks. I like yours, too. It's very...purple."

"It's actually Purrrple Passion. With three Ps."

"Your favorite number."

"No. Twenty-seven."

"Well I was one-third right."

"Nerp. One-ninth."

I cursed my stupidity. I was getting sucked into Fernville. I smiled and focused my attention on the teacher. She had slowed her carefully rehearsed speech and was sort of watching the exchange between Fern and me. When I stopped, she looked back down at the syllabus in her hand and continued on.

"What class do you have next?" Fern whispered.

"Trig."

"Oh. I took that last year. I have Calculus."

I blinked in surprise. If I had a horrible subject it would be anything math related. Everything else I did fine at, but I excelled in science. Except for physics which was mostly math. I tended to rush everything and make careless mistakes. I cringed at the thought of taking calculus. My respect for Fern rose just a hair.

Maybe she's weird because she's gifted.

I could see that. I could also see her pushing on the pull door and setting fire to the neighbor's house, but some gifted kids were a different breed.

I listened to the teacher. It took all of five minutes before Fern hit me in the temple with a crumpled piece of paper. I closed my eyes and took a deep breath before covering it with my hand. It had somehow spun to a stop on top of my desk instead of bouncing to the floor.

I turned my head to give her a dirty look, but she was making unwrapping motions with her hands. Either that, or upside-down swimming jelly fish motions. I was betting the former.

I moved the paper behind the person sitting in front of me and slowly began to open it while maintaining my stare at the teacher. I *really* didn't want to get caught with a note from Fern. If she made me stand up in front of the class and read it… Who the hell knew what it said.

I got it open and flattened it out in front of me.

What's your phone number? Write it on here and throw it back at me.

I wanted to throw it back at her. After I wrapped it around a brick. Maybe a hand grenade. Plutonium would be nice, too. The last thing I wanted to give her was my phone number.

Why?

I hated the voice in my head.

I looked up at Fern. She was staring at the piece of paper in my hands, waiting. I can freely admit, I wasn't the nicest guy in the world. I wasn't lying when I told her I didn't like people. Mostly because they didn't like me. I was different. I preferred to be alone and read. I preferred not to do stupid things with friends. Hell, even back in Chicago I only had two or three people I talked to more than once or twice a day. I didn't even like talking to my parents. Give me my computer, my video games, and a book, and I was happy. Not writing my phone number down would be tantamount to just being a douche. I knew nothing good would come of it, but…

I sighed and put my digits down, wadded it up, set it in front of her when Miss Jacoby wasn't looking, and then leaned my head on my hand. I began flipping through the book on my desk, seeing what we would be covering over the coming year, when my phone vibrated in my backpack by my foot. I ignored it, *not* wanting to get caught with it in class. My last school had been guerilla warfare sneaky on the battle against student cell usage. I had no idea how Woodrow Wilson High was on the subject. I even glanced around the room and didn't see a single cell in the hands of any of the students. Except for Fern. She was tapping away merrily on her screen.

The buzzing at my feet kept droning on and on. Luckily, nobody around seemed to hear it but me. I vowed to put it on silent between classes.

Fern reached over with her Converse-covered foot and nudged me in the thigh, waving her cell at me. I pointed at the teacher. She shrugged and typed something else.

"Fern. Put it away," the teacher called out from the front of the room.

Fern sighed and rolled her eyes, putting it in her hoodie.

Ten minutes later, the bell rang. Thankfully.

"I'm heading to class. Answer me when you can," Fern said sadly and headed toward the door. It was then I noticed she didn't have a single book or even a bag with her.

"Where the hell did she get the pen and paper?" I whispered as she left.

She stopped in the doorway, turned, and gave me a slow wink.

A chill ran down my spine. Shaking my head, I stuffed my book in my bag and grabbed my schedule. It had the class number for Trig. I just needed to figure out where the hell it was.

"Dane, got a moment?"

"Sure, Miss Jacoby," I said, and headed to her desk.

She waited until the last of the students filed out the door before looking up at me. "I..." She paused, gathering her thoughts.

"Did I do something wrong?"

"No! I'm sorry. It's Fern. I'm sure you noticed there's something *different* about her?"

I nodded. "From the moment I met her, and she accused me of looking at her ass."

"Yes. That's Fern. Our *normal* Fern. Standoffish, sometimes belligerent, always disrespectful. However, she is also one of the most brilliant students I have *ever* taught."

"Do you want me to stay away from her? Because I have absolutely no problem doing that..."

"Kind of the opposite, but..."

"But what?"

19

"I've never seen her *talk*. No. That's not the word I'm looking for. She talks at people all the time. Not hearing, not caring. I've never seen her take an *interest*, and I mean that in the vaguest sense of the word, in anybody before…you. I saw her pathetic attempt at a note passing. I let it go. I also ignored your cell phone going off twenty times. I'm assuming that was her?"

"Yeah. She asked for my number. I didn't know she was going to start texting in class."

"Thank you for not answering. Keep it on silent next time."

"Planning on it. Sorry about that."

"You seem like a nice kid, Dane. Be nice to her if you can. I'm sure she could use a friend. If she becomes too much for you to handle, let me know, and I'll move your seat and have a talk with her."

Warning bells and a claxon sounded even in the farthest reaches of my mind. I opened my mouth to say, "Oh, hell no," but it came out as more of a, "Sure. I'll be her friend."

I wanted to slap the shit out of myself, but the smile spreading across Miss Jacoby's face stayed my hand.

"You *are* a nice kid, Dane. I'm glad Fern met you."

"Yeah…" I chuckled. "Me, too."

CHAPTER 3

I didn't know enough about the food at Woodrow Wilson to know if I needed to bring my own lunch or not. I figured I'd give the cafeteria a shot for the first day.

I would *never* eat in the cafeteria again.

I was offended by the food on my tray. Horrified and afraid. I think it was supposed to be pizza. The cheese was clear, the salad looked like somebody had scraped the toppings off a burger, and the Jell-O was liquid. Mostly.

My hands were shaking as I slowly lowered my tray to the empty table. I was afraid it might explode and kill everyone in the room. Once it had settled and the Jell-O stopped shaking, I sighed, sat on the bench, and put my backpack on the ground beneath me.

I poked the pizza. It growled back at me. Fearing for my life, I stabbed it with my plastic fork, pinning it to the Styrofoam plate beneath it.

"I wouldn't eat that."

I looked up and felt the nerve running from my forehead to my spine twitch in apprehension at Fern sitting down across from me. "Hey, Fern."

"Did you want to look at my butt before I sat?"

"What?"

"Last chance…"

"Fern! I don't want to look at your butt, okay?"

"You don't like my ass?"

21

"I'm sure it's quite lovely. But, and I don't know if you noticed this or not, we are at *school*."

"Oh. You're afraid of getting in trouble. I see. I can show it to you later if you want."

"I… Whatever. Eat."

She picked the pizza off my tray and bit into it. "Yummers."

"I thought you said I shouldn't eat that?"

"I meant the Jell-O. That shit's nasty. Who the hell eats yellow Jell-O? Even the name is weird. Yel-low Jell-O. Doesn't exactly roll off the tongue, does it?"

"Kind of. Yes. It does. It even rhymes, Fern."

"Does it? I hadn't noticed."

I rubbed my eyes and did some breathing exercises. After the red left my vision, I picked up my salad and grabbed the fork Fern tossed on the tray, shoveling a bit in my mouth. Luckily it tasted better than it looked.

"You want some of this pizza?"

"No. You can have it. It didn't look that appetizing anyway."

"Suit yourself. I'll share my lunch with you if you want."

"What lunch?"

She tossed the crust on the tray, reached under her hoodie, and pulled out a carefully wrapped lunch box. She untied the knot on the top and revealed an ornately carved bento box and chopsticks. She unhooked the tie and opened it up, revealing two trays. One had been packed with rice and sprinkled with dried plum. The other one was filled with rolled sushi, chicken cutlets sliced neatly, and even hot dogs carved like squid.

"You had that under your hoodie this whole time?"

"Where else would I keep it. Not like it would fit in my pants."

I wasn't going there. Nope.

Her lunch, however, looked and smelled delicious. "You sure you don't mind?"

"No way. You gave me your pizza. It's only fair."

"You stole it, but sure. Let's go with that."

"If you really wanted it, you would have stopped me."

She did have a valid point. I was almost grateful when she removed it from my sight. "So how was calculus?"

She picked up the chopsticks and speared one of the octopuses, dipping it in a small container of soy sauce, and bringing it to her lips. She neatly bit the head off. It was the first time I'd noticed her teeth. They were extraordinarily white, and perfect. For the most part. Her canines, instead of curving downward, were more pronounced and curved neatly to the sides. It was kind of cute.

She watched me watching her. A tiny smirk twisted the corner of her mouth upward as her opposite eyebrow lifted. "What?"

I coughed, embarrassed. "I asked you how calculus was."

"Oh. Boring. How was Trig?" She sounded almost normal.

"Hard. I kind of suck at math."

"Well, if you ever need a tutor, let me know. Maths are easy."

I noticed she pluralized it. Like someone from the UK would. I didn't comment on it, though. I didn't want to know. "Sure. Thanks."

"Here, have a bite," she said, and held out the other half of the squid dog.

I almost hesitated, but I didn't want to hurt her feelings, so I grabbed it between my teeth and pulled it off the end of her chopsticks. I'd never been a fan of hot dogs in any shape, but it was quite tasty, plump and juicy. Especially with the soy sauce.

"That's pretty good."

23

"Wait till you try the sushi. Have some of the rice. Use your fork, though. It's a bitch with chopsticks."

I reached for my fork and happened to glance up. Everyone at the tables around us had stopped talking and were staring at us. Kind of like in the movies, when two people are dancing, and the music stops and the lights come on, and everybody is standing around watching. Except we weren't dancing. We were just sitting alone at an entire table in the lunchroom, eating. Without music. I could feel every set of eyes in the room boring into me. A wave of queasiness washed over me as my hands started to shake.

"What's wrong?"

"Um. Don't look, but everyone is staring at us..."

Not only *did* she look. She stood up and stared down every table. Everyone turned around or looked at their food. She *humphed* and sat back down, stabbing a piece of sushi.

"Silly mortals. Need to mind their own bee's wax."

"Silly mortals?" I laughed a little.

"I know, right? Can't keep 'em, and you can't eat 'em."

"Last one got stuck in my teeth. Took me a week to get it out," I said, playing along.

"Ugh. That's the worst. They're so *stringy*."

"And high in cholesterol."

She chuckled, nibbling on her sushi and staring at my empty tray. I slid it out of the way. Her gaze traveled to my eyes. I'd avoided looking into people's eyes my entire life. Whenever someone talked to me, I'd watched their lips as they spoke. I'm sure it was deeply rooted in my dislike of conversing, but it was just something that came naturally. I hadn't even thought about my little quirk until my eyes met hers. They were a stunning shade of blue. I didn't even know irises could be that color. Almost silver.

"You have pretty eyes, Fern."

Her fingertips shot up and covered her mouth. "I forgot something. I need to go. Finish the food," she said, and stood, nearly running for the cafeteria door.

I watched her run away and cursed myself. I shouldn't have said that. In fact, I hadn't meant to. When I was around her, my inside and outside voices got a little jumbled up. I shook my head, dumping the contents of the bento onto my empty plate and packing it up neatly. I emptied my tray, grabbed the stuff and left, ignoring the stares that had resumed as soon as she left.

I carried it from class to class, hoping to run into her again, but I didn't see her for the rest of the day. Before lunch, I would have pumped my fist and shouted, "Yeah!" As I exited the school, bento in hand, I felt a little sad and wondered if my compliment had been out of line, or if she was conscientious about her eyes.

Maybe she thought I was being sarcastic?

I had no clue. I hardly understood people. Girls were another creature altogether. They needed to come with PDF files containing warnings, labels, and instructions.

My mother's Cougar coughed to a stop in the nearly empty parent pickup line. I got off the metal bench and climbed into the front seat, fastened my seatbelt, and made the sign of the cross.

"What's that?" She nodded at the lunch box in my hand.

"Hi, Mom. Great to see you, too. It's a lunch box."

"Don't get smart. Not like you were sweet this morning. How was school? Why do you have a lunchbox?"

She took her foot off the break and we rumbled off, a single solitary muffler fart echoing in the parking lot. "It's a friend of mine's."

She hit the brake again, and we skidded to a stop.

"Say that again?"

"It's a friend of mine's," I said, and rolled my eyes.

"You made a *friend*?"

25

"Well, she sort of didn't leave me a choice."

"*She*?"

"Mom. Can you please just drive?"

"Not until you promise to tell me all about her."

"Fine."

She squealed, hitting the gas and surging forward. "What's her name?"

"Fern."

"She's a plant? I don't need to send you back to the therapist, do I?"

"No, Mom. She's a real girl with a real lunch box. Fern is her last name. Lucy is her first."

"Is she cute?"

"Most of the time. She's super smart and super weird. But, she kind of grows on you."

"I'm shocked. My baby boy is growing up."

"I'm a freaking *senior*, Mom. Could you please not?"

"Not what?"

"Never mind. Just get us home."

"The moving truck came this morning. All your boxes are in your room."

"Thanks. I'll unpack when we get home."

"You got homework?"

"It's the first day. The teachers weren't that cruel."

CHAPTER 4

I shoved most of my clothes into my rickety dresser. It had seen better days, and I almost left it in Chicago. Mom begged me to take it for now and would get me another when we had a bit more money. By the time that happened, I would probably be graduated from college, have a full-time job, and a family of my own. I silently cursed my father for the hundredth time for moving in with his secretary.

Mom was so angry, she basically didn't want anything from him. She signed the divorce papers without a second glance and dropped them in the mail. She did get child support, that was mandatory, but she didn't try to get anything from him. The house we lived in was rented, so she didn't even get any money from splitting the assets. Dad had asked me to stay in Chicago, but I think that was to get out of paying child support. I told him what he could go do to himself. As tempting as it was to stay in Chicago, I couldn't abandon Mom, not after the way he'd screwed her and our family.

I caught myself almost punching the wall from thinking about him. Slamming the dresser drawer shut instead, I turned around and surveyed my new domain. The house was ancient, but clean. Small, but cute. Mom had gotten a little bit of money from Gramma and Grampa, and used it for first, last, and security. Good Buy even helped pay for the move.

Everything was unpacked, not that I had a ton of stuff. The only things I hadn't brought were my myriad of posters on the walls of my own room. The new one was completely barren. There would be time to decorate it later. I lay on my bed and stared at my ceiling. My hand touched my backpack, where I'd unceremoniously dumped it when we got home. I unzippered it and pulled out my phone.

Thirty-two messages from Fern. I was pretty sure most of them were from Lit class, but I scrolled through them anyway. The questions ranged from, "Do you have any birthmarks?" to "What's your favorite flavor of sausage?" I found myself laughing as I made my way through their insanity. The final one was the one that kind of made me feel like a selfish shit. *Hey, Dane, I'm sorry if I bothered you today. Would it be okay if I talked to you tomorrow?*

Sorry, just looked at my phone. It's totally okay. I was worried about you after you ran away. You okay?

I turned my ringer back on and scrolled through my newsfeed. Most of it was politics and politically based bullshit. I only slipped in for the gaming news. I almost jumped when my phone went off in my hand.

Who is this?

I chuckled. Typical Fernese response. *Your friend, Dane.*

Oh. The butt guy.

Yes, I answered, grinning at my phone.

My phone stayed silent for a few minutes. Maybe I shouldn't have acknowledged my imaginary butt fetish. It finally *dinged* again, and I opened my messages back up. She'd sent a picture…

I began to sweat nervously as I clicked it to see what the hell it was she sent. It rendered slowly. I was still on cell service and not Wi-Fi. Mom had set up the electric and the water. Cable and internet would be tomorrow. Finally, the picture appeared. I sighed in relief. She had taken a picture of her butt, but she was still wearing jeans.

Show me yours.

I almost ignored the request. The idea of snapping a picture of my butt and sending it to a girl I'd just met... It kind of turned me on. I'm not going to lie. I smirked and rolled over on my stomach, shooting a picture of my ass over my shoulder. Without a second thought, I hit send.

Perv, she sent back. But then it was followed by a winky face.

That's me.

What are u doing?

Unpacking

Want some company?

Mom's home. See you tomorrow?

But I'm bored.

Mom would freak if I had a girl over. She's not...normal.

And I am?

Fern had a good point. No way in hell was I introducing Fern to my mother, though. She might call the cops if Fern started licking the paint or something equally weird.

Please?

I narrowed my eyes. *Hang on. Let me ask.*

I walked through the house until I found my mother in the kitchen, unpacking the utensils. "Need some help?"

"No. I unpacked almost the whole house while you were at school. This is the last room, and you don't know where I want everything."

"Sorry I wasn't home to help."

"It's okay. I still have the rest of the week off. I can putter while you're at school. Don't forget, you're bussing it next week and every week after that."

"I know. Cheese-wagon."

"Sorry. You know I'd get you a car if we could afford it."

"I know."

"What do you want? You're being way too nice right now..."

"Mother, thou hast cleft my heart in twain."

"I don't have any money."

I laughed and shook my head. "Remember that friend I mentioned, well more like you grilled me about, making me very uncomfortable? Would it be okay if she came over to hang out for a bit?"

"Sure. Keep your door open. Do I need to go buy you condoms for when I'm not around to protect your chastity?"

The utter look of shock and dismay I gave her was her reward. She cackled gleefully and continued unpacking. "Please, for the love of God and all that is holy, refrain from saying anything *remotely* like that while Fern is here, and for the rest of forever. I'll be in my room. Until Friday at least, when I can look at you again."

I walked away, ignoring her diabolical laughter.

Come over. I texted Fern my address.

Two minutes later, the doorbell echoed ominously through the house, like it wasn't getting enough electricity. The chimes sounded warped and…evil?

In the distance, I heard my mother unchaining the door and pulling it open. "Hi! You must be Fern. Dane told me all about you. I'm Mrs. Evans."

"Hi. I'm Fern. I'm a Scorpio and like to take long walks through dimly lit cemeteries on foggy nights."

I ran to the front door before the conversation got weird. Weirder. "Fern!" I gasped as she came into view. She gave me a little wave around my mother. "Mom, Fern. Fern, this is my mother. Bye, Mom."

I motioned to Fern to follow me back to my room, ignoring the look of confusion on my mother's face.

Finally, Mom snapped out of it. "I'm going to order Chinese. Are you kids hungry?"

"Yes! I'll have beef with broccoli," I said, and looked at Fern. "Do you like Chinese?"

She nodded and smiled at me. "Yes."

"What do you want?"

"Do you have a menu?"

"Not on me, no. What do you normally get?"

"Moo goo gai pan."

"Fern wants moo goo gai pan, Mom."

"Okay. I'll holler when it's here."

"Would you like me to order? I speak fluent Chinese."

"Huh?" My mother and I were hardly *ever* in sync. You could count the number of times we had the same thought on exactly two fingers. That might have been the first time in the history of forever that we said the same thing at the same time.

"*Wǒ shuō pǔtōnghuà.*"

I wasn't sure if she said, "I speak Chinese," or insulted my mother. Either way, I stared in disbelief. "That's okay, Fern. I'm sure my mother can handle ordering combination platters…"

"Okay. Combination!" She turned back to Mom. "Can I have an eggroll, fried rice, and hot and sour soup with mine, please?"

"Sure…"

For the first time in my life, I saw my mother totally unsure of how to deal with a situation. She stared at Fern and slowly opened her mouth to surely let loose with a barrage of a million questions.

"Thanks, Mom!" I shouted and reached down, grabbing Fern's hand and slowly but surely walking her to my room.

I almost closed the door behind us, but remembered my mother's warning about leaving it open. I was just grateful to be in my sanctuary.

I smiled at Fern. "Welcome to my house. How did you get here so quick?"

She pointed at my wall. "I live two houses over."

"No shit."

"I went before school."

I resisted the urge to slap my forehead. "That's more information than I ever needed to know." I sat down at my desk, letting her sit on my bed. She jumped on the mattress, spun in a circle three times, and then lay down on her side, facing me and propping her head up on her hand.

She still wore her black hoodie, but she had changed out of her jeans and was wearing a skin-tight pair of black leggings. I tried very hard to focus on her face. With her curled up in a little ball, they had become quite transparent...

"So... You speak Chinese?"

"Nerp."

I groaned. "Why did you tell my mother you were fluent?"

"*Wǒ cóng bù shuōhuà. Dàn wǒ zhīdào rúhé.*"

"Huh?"

"I never speak, but I know how."

"So, you *know* Chinese."

"*Da. Russkiy, a takzhe.*"

"Was that Russian?"

"*Sí.*"

"Spanish. Let me guess. Twenty-seven languages. And you are fluent in all of them..."

She smiled and nodded.

"Is there anything else I should know about you?"

She smiled again and shrugged. "If I think of anything, I'll let you know."

She rolled on her back and stretched. I turned around and faced my desk. She giggled behind me. "You like my pants."

She didn't ask. She told me I did. She wasn't wrong. "They're very um...stretchy."

"Comfortable, too. I wore them in case you wanted to look at my butt."

"Well, thank you for not sending the picture wearing those. I might have gotten arrested."

I felt her breath on the back of my neck. She had moved from the bed without making a single sound. I gasped when she gently scratched me down the back of my neck with a sharp nail. It didn't hurt. It kind of felt...good. Too good.

"Fern..."

"Yes, Dane?"

"What are you doing?"

"Seeing if you like me."

I sighed, refusing to turn around. For several reasons. "Why?"

"Curiosity. I've never really talked to a boy before. You're the first one who didn't annoy me."

Lucky me.

"You are lucky."

I blinked in surprise. She might have just been making a generalized statement, but I shuddered briefly. It was almost as if she could read my thoughts. Then I groaned inwardly. That would be impossible.

Fern turned my desk chair around slowly. I let her do it, moving my knees out of the way of my desk. She turned me completely around, facing her. "Want to go for a walk?"

She sat down in my lap and leaned back against me. I shifted, centering her weight so the chair didn't slide out from beneath us or topple over. It wasn't the greatest desk chair in the world.

"What are you doing?"

"Standing is uncomfortable."

"And sitting on my lap is comfortable?"

"Aye."

The smell of her shampoo wafted over me, and the heat of her back pressed against my chest. Her slight frame fit perfectly in my lap. I gripped the arms of the chair to keep my hands still and not touch anything inappropriately.

She tilted her head back and looked into my eyes. "Walk?"

"Um. My mom ordered dinner. After?"

She nodded. "I forgot."

Her stomach growled. Not surprisingly, as she had run out of the cafeteria, not eating her lunch. She looked down at the offending organ, and I chuckled. "Hungry?"

"Yes."

"Dane," my mom said from the hallway outside my room.

I wrapped my arms around Fern and stood up, turning around and pretending to look for something on my desk just as my mom walked into the room. "Yeah?"

"Dinner will be here shortly. What are you two up to? Sorry, the cable isn't on."

"It's okay. I was trying to find a board game or something to occupy us until dinner came. Then we were going to go for a walk."

"That sounds like…fun. And unlike you."

"You're funny, Mother."

"I'll holler when dinner's here."

"Thanks."

I sighed when she exited my domain.

"We're playing a board game?"

I almost laughed at Fern's confused expression. "No. I just didn't want my mother to see you sitting in my lap. I never would have heard the end of it."

"Why?"

"Because I've never had a girlfriend before."

I realized I screwed up when her eyes widened. She sat down on the edge of my bed and looked like she was going to cry. "Is that what I am?"

"Well, you are my friend and you are a girl. It's not like we're dating…"

"Oh." She sniffled and rubbed her hands together nervously.

"Do you even like me?"

She nodded. Almost vigorously. "Yes. I have no desire to see you come to harm."

"Well, that's good. Thanks." I shook my head at her choice of words.

"I wish you a safe future, as well. How about we take things slowly, see how they go? We're not in a rush. I mean we did just meet like ten hours ago."

"Okay."

I breathed out a sigh of relief. If I were to be totally honest, Fern was cute. Adorable even. I could *not,* however, ever see me dating her. Friends, yes. Girlfriend, no. She took quirky to an entirely different plane of existence.

She was staring at my stomach and nibbling on her thumb, thinking about God knew what. I probably would have been better off not knowing. Ever.

She is damn cute, though.

She looked up at me and smiled.

The doorbell rang.

"Kids! Dinner!"

I held out my hand to Fern. She grabbed it and rubbed her face against the back of it. Like a cat would. I laughed and ran my hand over her silky purple hair, half expecting her to start purring.

"I was helping you up."

"Why? I can stand with no problems."

"I know. It's polite and a physical way of saying that it's time to go eat."

"Oh. You just wanted to touch me. You're perverted."

I sighed and let it go. "You caught me."

She smiled and tugged on my hand. I pulled her to her feet, a little shocked at how light she was. I'd noticed when she sat on my lap. I wasn't athletic, but I had absolutely no trouble standing up with her sitting on me earlier.

"Come on. Let's get some food into that stomach of yours before it chews a hole through you."

I started walking toward the dining room and let go of her hand. She didn't. I settled for putting my hand down low, hoping that my mother wouldn't notice. Maybe Fern would let go before then.

"Hurry up," Mom said, and set everything out on the counter separating the kitchen from the dining room. "Chopsticks or forks?" She looked at Fern, already knowing my preference.

"Chopsticks, please."

We grabbed everything and set it down on the table. I put Fern's food across from me, but she slid it back to the empty seat next to me. Mom stifled a giggle, earning a frown from me. Instead of sitting at the head of the table on the other side of me, she put her food across the table from the two of us.

"So, where do you live, Fern?" Mom started with the polite conversation while I popped the lid off my beef and broccoli. Sniffing at it tentatively, I hoped it would be good. The sauce smelled delicious, at least. I popped a bigger hunk of beef in my mouth and started chewing. I made appreciative noises. It wasn't bad at all.

"Two houses down the street."

"Really? Isn't that…convenient."

I could tell she didn't mean it. I made a mental bet with myself that she would be calling an alarm company tomorrow to have the window in my room monitored.

"Very," Fern added merrily.

I doubled the bet in my head.

"Do you take the bus to school?"

Fern shook her head. "No. I like to walk."

"Oh, that's perfect. Stop by in the morning and pick up Dane. You can walk together."

"It's like two miles, Mom…"

"How will you ever survive?"

"Plus, Fern is late every day."

"Leave five minutes earlier. You'll be fine."

I growled and stabbed a piece of broccoli with my chopstick. "You'll walk with me?" Fern sounded ecstatic.

"Guess so."

"He'd be delighted to, Fern. Once we get settled in, you should have your parents over for dinner. Be nice to get to know the neighbors."

"It's just my mom. And she's in Oak Hills Psychiatric Ward for a few months…"

I dropped my chopsticks.

"Oh, my. Is she okay?" Mom sounded shocked. Me, not so much.

"She had another breakdown. Doctors say she should be fine once they level out her medication levels."

"And you're all by yourself?"

"Yes. Technically my aunt is staying with me, but I haven't seen her in a couple of weeks."

"Oh, dear Lord. If you need anything, please just come over."

"Thank you."

Without my noticing, Fern had finished her dish, her rice, and her soup. I'd been too busy picking at mine and praying the conversation didn't get weird. Once I heard about her mom and her always being alone, I lost the rest of my appetite. I put the cover on the rest of my food to go into the fridge. A move that didn't go unnoticed by my mother. She probably felt the same. When you think life is rough, there is always someone with it rougher than you.

"Thank you for dinner," Fern said politely.

"Have you been eating enough lately?" Mom slipped into full on Mominator mode.

"Yes. I go shopping and make dinners and lunches."

"That reminds me, I have your lunch box. You should see the food she makes, Mom," I added, trying to keep the conversation on normal topics.

"Hey, don't be eating her food. I gave you money for your lunch account."

"Yeah. I'll use it for drinks and bring my lunch from now on. The cafeteria food isn't fit for swine consumption."

"That good, huh?"

"Worse."

"I can make more lunch," Fern chimed in.

"No! The boy can take care of himself."

"I don't mind. He eats with me anyway. It's not hard to make a little more. I even have another set of chopsticks."

"You make a bento every day?"

She nodded. "Tomorrow is rolled omelet day."

Fern was an anime character. She had to be. It explained so much…

"*Arigatō*," I said to test the theory.

"*Dōitashimashite*," she answered without batting an eyelash. "*Anata wa nihongo o hanasu*."

"What?" I loved anime, but I hadn't understood a word of what she said.

"What language was that?" My mother was in awe.

"Um. Japanese?"

"Oh. Thought it sounded familiar."

Mom shot me an astonished look. I nodded knowingly. "She speaks twenty-seven languages, Mom."

Mom whistled. "No wonder she can't keep track of which one is which. I'm no expert, but it sounded perfect."

I ruffled Fern's hair. "She promised to help me with my Trig homework, too."

"Oh, thank God."

I felt Fern tense under my hand. I removed it, but she grabbed it and put it back on her head. Mom laughed.

I yawned and arched my back, stretching a bit. It had been a long day, and I was tired. The thought of going on a walk kind of didn't appeal to me. Especially if I was going to be running a marathon in the morning just to get to school.

Fern squeezed my hand. "Are you tired?"

"Yeah. A little."

"We can skip the walk. I have something I need to do anyway."

"Okay. Are you sure?"

She smiled. "Thank you again for dinner, Mrs. Evans. You have a lovely home," she said and stood, gathering up her empty containers.

"Leave the mess, Fern. I'll make the boy clean it up."

CHAPTER 5

The sweltering heat woke me up from my restless dreams. I'd been running through the forest being chased by a gigantic black panther, but that wasn't what woke me up. It was the heat making me sweat under the comforter. I flung it off me and almost screamed.

Fern was curled up next to me in my bed.

"*Fern?*" I hissed, touching her shoulder.

She rolled to her back, her open hoodie flaring out around her like a pair of dark wings. The sunlight filtered through my window and illuminated her like a dark angel. She wore a very thin white T-shirt, and I sincerely doubted she had anything on under that. If she had pants, she wasn't wearing them. She had on a pair of simple white cotton underwear. Her skin looked like white porcelain, just a few shades darker than her garments, and didn't have a single blemish, freckle, or mark. My boxers became uncomfortable.

I looked up from her lack of clothing to her face. She was watching me. "Sorry. I got here early so I snuck in through your window and took a nap."

"Pants?" It was the only word my addled brain could manage.

"Nobody sleeps in pants."

"Some people do."

"I don't. I kept my panties on, though. In case your mom came in."

"Thanks. Big difference. Quick death verses slow tortuous death."

"Your mom would care?"

"She'd beat me with a frying pan."

"I'd protect you."

"Thanks?"

She rolled on her side, wrapping her arms around me and burying her face in my shoulder. Her breath sent shivers up my skin and… If my boxers weren't already ripped, I'm sure they would be by the time I got the nerve to look.

The knock on my door took care of that, quick. "Dane! Time to get up," Mom shouted through the door. Thank God she didn't come in.

"Yeah… I'm already up." *Or, I was.*

"Well, get ready in case Fern gets here early."

If you only knew. "Will do, Mom."

"You okay? You sound funny. Never mind, I don't wanna know," she mumbled just loud enough for me to hear.

"Ew. Mom. Gross," I whispered.

"Does she think you're touching yourself?"

"Fern. Don't ever say that again. Ever."

"Why?"

"Because. Some things should *never* be talked about. Ever, ever, ever."

"I don't understand. Everybody touches themselves. I do it all the time."

"Fern! No," I hissed, mentally pleading for my mother to knock on my door again.

"What?"

"Never mind. We need to get dressed. You need to sneak back out the window and knock on the front door."

"Okay," she said, and slid down to the foot of the bed, carefully standing up. *Finally*, I looked at her butt. I hadn't meant to, but her hoodie didn't cover the bottom half of it. Her panties had crept up, too, from sliding down the mattress. She slowly turned her head, noticed where I was looking, and smiled. "Perv."

Damn it all to hell. Busted.

She slowly reached behind her and grabbed her panties, pulling them down and covering her cheeks. I didn't know if I should be happy or cry.

When she bent over to grab her pants off the floor, I nearly passed out, but was grateful she had adjusted herself before bending over. It might have killed me.

I groaned instead.

Fern's faint chuckle rang in my ears.

"You did that on purpose," I whispered.

She just shrugged, tucking her shirt into her jeans and sitting down to put her shoes on. It would be a few more minutes before I could get out from under the strategically placed pillow I had hastily thrown over my lap.

I noticed that my window was still wide open. I hadn't noticed if there was a screen on it before or not. If so, it was gone now. My room dropped in temperature. It was a bit chilly outside.

But I was so hot I woke up?

I shrugged. Maybe I was getting sick.

Fern finished tying her shoes and nimbly dove through the window, not making a sound.

"What the hell?"

I scrambled to the end of my bed and looked outside, but she was already walking toward the front door. I jumped out of bed, grabbed a clean pair of jeans and tugged them on. I remembered to slap on some deodorant before tossing on a semi-clean T-shirt and grabbing a pair of socks. I'd left my shoes by the front door.

The bell rang.

"Dane! Fern's here. I told you to get up!"

"I am up! Just gotta brush my teeth. Would you let her in?"

I heard the front door open and some muffled greetings while I jumped into the bathroom and did just that. By the time I finished, Mom and Fern were sitting on the couch and drinking coffee.

"Morning, Fern."

"Morning, Dane."

"You ready to go?"

"Not unless you want to get to school thirty minutes early. Plus, your mom gave me *coffee*."

I shook my head, wondering at the wisdom of giving Fern caffeine. I shrugged and grabbed a Coke out of the fridge. They could caffeinate their way, and I would caffeinate mine.

"You don't like coffee?"

I shook my head at Fern. "It's gross. Unless it's iced with a bunch of cream and sugar. Some caramel. Maybe vanilla. Never pumpkin, though. That's gross, too."

"I've never had it any other way than this." She held up her steaming mug. Once I got close enough, I saw her drinking it black.

"You want to try it with some cream and sugar?"

"No. I like it like this."

"Well, I'll take you to Starbucks after school. I'll get you an iced macchiato or something. Is there one around here?"

"I don't know. I make it at home."

"I'll check on my phone. If you want to go?"

"Sure."

"Crap. I forgot to make some lunch. Finish your coffee."

"I made enough. Don't worry."

I'd seen her in just her underwear a few minutes ago. She didn't grab anything before she dove out the window. "Where? You don't have a bookbag. Did you leave it at home?"

She reached under her hoodie and pulled out a wrapped bento box. I looked over at the counter and saw the one she had forgotten to take with her last night.

How many boxes does she own? Where the hell was she hiding this one?

I stared at her for a moment.

She had to have stashed it on the porch or something. She grabbed it when she rang the bell. That had to be it. I'm glad Mom didn't see it or anything.

I shrugged, promising myself I would ask her about it later.

"So, yeah. Dane's dad moved in with his secretary. He wanted Dane to stay in Chicago, but he was pretty pissed off at his dad, so he moved here with me, thankfully. I probably wouldn't have taken the promotion if he insisted on staying," Mom said, resuming their conversation.

"He abandoned you?" Fern's eyebrows knitted together.

"Yep. I should have known after being married for eighteen years that he would never grow up. Love makes you stupid."

"Does it?"

"Sometimes."

"And you're full of crap, Mother. I did insist on staying. You told me to suck it up and pack my crap," I added, joining in and sipping on my Coke.

"I knew you didn't mean it."

I rolled my eyes. I should have asked her two-hundred-and-thirty-*eight* times. Then maybe she would have gotten the hint.

Is it so bad here?

I ignored myself. I hated it when I was being logical.

Fern downed her coffee. I looked at her in shock. *How the hell did she do that?* It had been steaming just a moment ago. Even Mom looked from her mug to Fern's face, hoping for some sort of reaction.

"That was good. Thank you, Mrs. Evans."

"Oh, just call me Connie."

Fern nodded, and headed to the kitchen, putting her mug in the sink and running some water into it. "You ready?"

"Yeah," I answered, guzzling my Coke. I tossed the empty can into the bin in the kitchen and ran back to my room for my backpack. "Now I am," I said with a smile and opened the front door for her.

"No looking at my butt," she quipped as she exited in front of me. Out of spite I looked. Quickly. She didn't seem to notice.

"Have fun, kids."

I shut the door without answering her.

Fern headed down to the sidewalk, and I rushed to catch up to her, falling into stride next to her.

"Your mom is nice."

"She has her moments."

"Your dad deserves to be punished."

"Oh, I'm sure he will. I'm a firm believer in Karma."

"That's the thing about Karma, Dane. Sometimes you gotta give it a helping hand," she answered cryptically.

It felt kind of nice that she cared enough to be angry about the whole situation. God knows I was. I kind of hoped, every day, that his new girlfriend would cheat on him the way he did Mom. It would serve him right. "Thanks, Fern."

"For what?"

"Caring."

She reached over and grabbed my hand. Hers was hot, but not clammy like yesterday. The weather was still chilly, and I was almost grateful for the warmth.

∞ ∞ ∞

I sat in my usual seat in Trig. I could feel the stares of the people around me. I could hear their unasked questions.

46

Instead of acknowledging them, I opened my book and notebook, staring straight ahead.

Mr. Blake got up from his desk and flipped on the overhead projector. A formula I had no chance in hell of understanding appeared on the screen in the front of the classroom. I was pretty sure, that if improperly solved, a rift into hell would appear before me, and a horde of Latin-chanting demons would come swarming out to wreak havoc upon the world. I set my pen down on my notebook, determined to keep the world safe.

There was a tap on my shoulder, and then a folded note dropped into my lap. I palmed it and set it down on the desk in front of me, out of sight. As Blake was explaining, I unfolded the tattered sheet of notebook paper.

Are you really going out with that freak of nature?

Sighing, I crumpled it up and tossed it back over my shoulder.

Ten minutes later another fell back into my lap. I should have just picked it up and put it in my backpack or pocket and ignored it. Curiosity got the better of me and I opened it, the crinkles making reading difficult.

I heard she put a kid in the hospital at her last school.

This time, I kept it. I wasn't going to listen to half-assed rumors.

When the third one dropped over my shoulder, I turned around and shot the cheerleaderesque brunette a dirty look and slapped it down on her desk.

"What is going on?"

Mr. Blake had wandered over sometime during the note passing fiasco without my noticing. He grabbed the note off the desk. "Passing notes in class, Mr. Evans? Aren't you a little old for this?"

Great. He thinks I wrote it.

He cleared his throat.

"Valerie," he started, looking at the brunette who sat behind me. "I know I am dating Fern, but I can't keep my eyes off you. Would you go out with me? P.S. I can't believe how boring this class is. Mr. Blake is a gaseous windbag."

I felt the blood drain from my face. The entire class erupted into a cacophony of shrills, cheers, and laughter. My life was over. I'd been set up. I couldn't even be mad at Valerie. The depths she'd gone to setting up her elaborate burn had well surpassed epic proportions. She deserved some sort of medal.

And yet, I still want to staple her hair to the bulletin board.

"Dane, why don't you take this note to Dean Winchester and see how he feels about seniors passing notes in my class."

"Yes, sir."

The collective "Oooh" could probably be heard several classrooms away.

I shoved my stuff in my bag and headed out the door, not giving Valerie the satisfaction of seeing me angry. She had no idea how much I was used to shit like this. In my last school, this was a weekly occurrence. It had become one of my mother's foremost selling points on moving away.

By the time I got to the dean's office, he was standing in the doorway waiting for me. "Dane Evans?"

"Yes, sir," I said quietly and entered. He let the door close behind me.

"Not going to protest your innocence?"

"Probably wouldn't do any good, sir."

"Let me see the note, son."

I dug it out of my pocket and handed it to him.

"You have a notebook in that bag?"

I nodded, confusedly. "Yes?"

"Let me see it."

I unzipped my backpack and grabbed the first notebook I saw. It happened to be English Lit. "Here you go."

He took it, flipped open to the first page I had written notes on and held the piece of evidence next to it. He set the note on his desk and closed my notes. Then, he handed the spiral notebook back to me. "The bell should be ringing shortly. You can sit in the main office until your next class."

"I'm not in trouble?"

He shook his head. "I'm a hard-ass, son, but only to those who truly deserve it. You didn't write that note. It's plain as day. I'll be speaking to Mr. Blake...*and* Valerie Jones."

I blinked in disbelief. "Thank you, sir."

"Go on, son."

He didn't have to ask twice. I exited through his other door, the one leading into the office and took a seat on the padded green pleather bench by the door. Smiling, I pulled out the book I kept in my backpack just for such occasions

CHAPTER 6

I sat down at the cafeteria table and waited for Fern. I'd just about given up hope when I felt a pair of hot hands cover my eyes. "Guess who."

"Hmmm. Fern?"

"How'd you know?"

"Your hands. You have really hot hands."

Instead of walking around the table and sitting down there, she parked herself next to me and whipped out her bento. I wanted to look inside her hoodie one day, and not for nefarious purposes. She had to have some sort of holder sewn into the lining. It was probably why she wore the same one day after day.

"I do?"

"Yes."

"You sure you just don't have cold hands?"

"It's a possibility, but they felt hot when you covered my eyes, too."

"Maybe you just get turned on by me."

"That, I think, is more of a possibility than I would like to admit."

"It's my butt, isn't it?"

"It is." I smiled, playing along.

"I knew it."

She lifted the lid off the bento. True to her word, the main compartment was filled with rolled omelet. I'd watched anime all my life and always wondered if it tasted like a regular omelet. It was my time to find out.

Fern handed me a pair of chopsticks, and I speared one of them. "Dip it in soy." She opened the little container and held it out for me.

Dunking just the tip in, I bit it in half. Its sweetness caught me off guard, but with the saltiness of the soy, it blended perfectly. "Wow. That's good," I whispered.

She grinned and nibbled a piece, taking some of the rice, too. "How was Trig?"

"Fine," I lied.

She narrowed her eyes at me. "What happened?"

"Nothing. One of the cheerleaders tried to get me in trouble, but it backfired."

"You're not in trouble?"

"No. Dean Winchester actually figured out what happened within a minute."

She nodded slowly, but then lifted her head up and looked around. Valerie waltzed through the door giggling with a couple of her squad mates. I could feel the surge of anticipation as Fern made to jump up and confront her.

I put my hand on her thigh and held her still. "Don't. Winchester knows it was her. I don't want you getting in trouble."

She almost snarled. I swear, red swirled in her eyes. She blinked, and it faded away. Shaking my head, I looked away. I must have imagined it.

Valerie slowed by our table on the way to hers. "Have fun in the dean's office, newbie?"

"He was actually quite nice. Seemed to recognize the handwriting on the wall right away. He laughed it off and let me go. But not before he said he would have a word with Mr. Blake and the party responsible. Oh, wait. That was you, wasn't it?"

"Valerie Jones, please report to Dean Winchester's office. Valerie Jones," crackled over the intercom speaker in the cafeteria.

"I'm sure it's unrelated," I said casually.

"Screw off, freaks."

Her prank had been epic. But not nearly as epic as Winchester's timing. It couldn't have been more perfect. The entire cafeteria turned to watch her walk of shame.

The collective "Ooooh" resounded even louder in the open lunch room.

It was loud enough I almost missed hearing Fern whispering, "*Infirmati sunt et ceciderunt.*"

Valerie's scream echoed off the walls as she lurched forward, crashing down on the linoleum. Her friends rushed to help her up and gasped. She spun around holding her nose as blood gushed from her hand. Twenty people rushed forward handing her wads of napkins as she rushed out of the cafeteria.

"Oh, my God. I hope she's okay."

"Who?"

"Valerie. Did you see her bash her face on the floor?"

Fern shrugged. "Why do you hope she's okay? She's a bitch."

"I know. I just don't like to see people get hurt."

"I thought you were a fan of karma?"

"I am, to a point. Equal penalty for the wrong committed. Karma already bit her in the ass. Winchester didn't seem too happy with her. That was enough in my books. Bashing her face into the ground was a little overkill."

"That's not how karma really works. The punishment doesn't fit the crime. The punishment brings three times the price of the wrong. It's called the three-fold-law."

"Is that why you like the number three so much?"

She just shrugged. "Eat," she said changing the subject.

"You're kind of cute when you're all growly and protective of me," I whispered to her.

She blinked up at me, a piece of omelet dangling from her chopsticks and her mouth partially open, poised to take a bite. I snatched the omelet away from her and bit into it, grinning at her a little.

"You think I'm cute?"

I nodded, not seeing the harm in admitting it.

Sitting there eating bento, she leaned against me and put her head on my shoulder. "Dane…"

"Eat."

∞ ∞ ∞

Lockers are disgusting when your face is pressed against one. I felt like scrubbing my skin with alcohol and anti-biotic wipes. At least I could still breathe. The jock behind me had my shoulders pinned behind his big beefy arm, not my chest.

"You think this is funny, asshole? She got suspended for two days because you ratted her out!"

"Actually, yes. But not for the reasons you think. I find it funny because I *didn't* rat her out. The dean knew it was her before I even said anything. Secondly, she did it to herself and yet, you're still blaming me. Not surprised, though. You've probably had like, what? Five? Six concussions?"

The lockers zoomed away and then came rushing back. "I'm going to snap your spine, you little dick wad."

Before I could come back with a witty retort, he let me go. And not by choice, apparently. When I turned around, he was lying on the ground. Fern knelt on his chest, poised to punch him in the face.

"Get off me, you freak!"

"Fern," I said softly. "Thanks, but he's not worth it."

She was panting heavily. I wasn't sure if she was going to stop or not. Either way, she had saved me a lot of pain. I meant it when I said thanks. Now I just needed to figure out how a ninety-pound hellcat had pulled a two-hundred-plus jock off me and pinned him to the floor...

Ninja. She's a fricking ninja. Has to be. Probably from eating all those bento boxes.

"Okay," she said calmly and stood, dusting herself off. A circle of people had gathered around to watch the long-haired nerdy kid get his ass kicked. Instead, they saw the floor get mopped with Megadouche's head. I'd call it a win.

I took Fern's hand and calmly walked away, shaking inside. There was a collective gasp behind me. Time slowed as I spun to find a fist flying toward my head, but there was little I could do to stop it. Closing my eyes, there was the sound of flesh striking flesh, and a cry of pain that wasn't my own.

Still expecting the impact, I opened one eye to see what the holdup was. The fist had stopped mere inches from my face, impeded by a tiny little hand clutching it. The disbelief on the jock's face was priceless. The silence from the spectators around us, deafening. Before I could say *anything*, Fern twisted his arm and forced him to the ground.

Before she could do anything else, I gripped her shoulder. "Don't hurt him."

Again, I couldn't believe I was telling a five-foot-tall girl not to hurt a football player, yet here I was. I could see the look of disappointment on her face. She let go of his hand. He stayed on his knees, clutching his wrist.

"I have a game on Friday, you bitch."

Something primal welled up within me. I'd been set to let him go, but he opened his mouth. Without thinking, I kicked out, striking him directly in the nose. I'll admit it, I'm not the world's most masculine guy, but something inside me snapped. Pick on me all you want. Call me names, grind me into a locker. I don't care. Pick on someone I care about, and I may go down, but I will sure as hell take you with me.

The jock, whose name I didn't even know, crossed his eyes and fell to the ground, his nose gushing blood like the cheerleader he'd been getting revenge for. He landed with a wet thud. It was at that moment that I knew.

I had feelings for Fern...

Shit.

"What the hell is going on here?"

The crowd surrounding us scattered in an instant, leaving Jock, Fern, and I the only ones left. I looked down at the passed-out creep at our feet, and back up to Dean Winchester. I shrugged.

"Evans?"

"Yes, sir."

"Hello, Fern," he said with a pitiful sigh, squatting down to check on Jock. "It would seem you had a small altercation with Mister Johnson here. Care to tell me what happened?"

"I was protecting Dane."

He looked at Fern. "Of course, you were. What happened Evans?" He ignored her. I'm sure it wasn't out of spite, just to get to the truth that much faster. And probably with less of a headache.

"Truthfully, she's right. He was angry that his girlfriend got suspended for the thing earlier and blamed me. Thought I ratted her out. He had me pinned against the lockers, and Fern put him down on the ground. I told her to stop, and we were walking away, when he tried to sucker punch me from behind. Again, she saved my ass, blocking the punch and twisting his arm until he went down again. We were going to walk away *again,*" I stressed, "when he called Fern an uncouth name."

"What happened then?"

"I kicked him in the face."

"Protecting the honor of your girlfriend, Mr. Evans?"

I opened my mouth to protest, but then closed it and just nodded.

"Fern, you are free to go. Thank you for putting a stop to the fight. Mr. Evans, you and Mr. Johnson here are coming to my office."

I sighed, actually seeing this outcome. I had struck after the fight was over. Self-defense is one thing. Kicking a person when he was down... Not so much. I deserved it. But I wouldn't have done anything different. Not in a million years. That kick felt *good*.

"Shouldn't we call an ambulance, sir?"

"He'll be fine. He gets hit harder in the head every Friday."

CHAPTER 7

As soon as my mother escorted me from the school, she slapped me on the back of the head.

"On the second day? Really, Dane?"

"Would you have done it differently?"

"Yes! I would have made sure there were no teachers or witnesses."

I laughed. Sometimes Mom could be pretty cool.

"Well, at least you have two days to help me finish setting up the house. Call your father and tell him you got suspended if you want. He'll probably be proud of you."

"No thanks."

"Just saying. If you ever feel the need to talk to him, he's your father. I don't mind."

"Yes, you do, and so do I. I'm good."

She smiled, letting it go. "So, all that in there wasn't bullshit? Fern beat the guy up twice?"

I nodded in awe. "You should have seen her, Mom. She was like Superman. She stopped his punch with one hand."

"Do I need to tell you not to piss her off?"

"No, ma'am."

"Smart boy. So, she speaks twenty-seven languages and has a blackbelt in something."

"Yeah."

"So why did you kick him in the face? Were you showing off?"

"No. He called Fern a bitch."

"You should have kicked him twice. I think the dean felt bad he had to suspend you. He seems like a pretty level-headed guy. At least you're not that athletic kid. Suspended for two weeks."

"He probably would have gotten expelled if it weren't for the football coach."

"Sad but true."

We got into the car. Mom turned the key, and the engine started cranking but wouldn't catch. She tried three more times before the battery finally gave out, and the engine resorted to clicking instead of turning.

She sighed and leaned forward, pressing her forehead against the steering wheel and laughing. It was better than crying.

"Want to walk? It's a nice night," I said sarcastically.

"Yeah. I'll call a mechanic in the morning."

We got out and started walking. "Sorry, Mom."

"For?"

"Getting suspended."

"Meh. Can't really blame you for that one. Don't let it happen again, though."

"I won't."

"So, you like her, huh?"

"If you had asked me yesterday morning, I would have had you checked for drug use," I started. "If you had asked me last night, my answer would have been no. This morning would have been a maybe. Now it's a 'I think so'. Kind of weird, huh?"

"No. That's about normal."

"That's scary."

"You have no idea. Know what it took for me to realize I liked your father?"

"If your story involves sex or kissing in any way, shape, or form… I don't want to know."

My *mom* made gagging noises. "Hell no. I never want to think about that ever again. With your father, I mean."

"Ew. But continue."

"We were at a party. I told him I wasn't interested. He asked one of my friends which house and window were mine. My friend, being quite the prankster, gave him my address, but told him Grampa's window was mine. He stood below Dad's window for twenty minutes, singing Guns and Roses ballads and playing his guitar…"

"How'd that go?"

"Twenty-gauge filled with rock salt…"

"Ouch."

"Yeah. Your father couldn't sit for a month. But I thought it was sweet. We dated for two years before I broke down and said yes to getting married."

"Bet you're sorry you did."

"Not ever. I may want to punch him in the face, but if I had said no, I wouldn't have you."

"Yeah. I'm definitely a prize worth eighteen years of hell."

"Hey! You may be anti-social and quirky, but I wouldn't trade you for anyone."

"Thanks, Mom."

"You're welcome."

We walked in silence after that. Not an awkward silence, either. We had both said what needed to be said, and what we wanted to say. Mom even threw her arm over my shoulder and gave me a quick hug at one point. I didn't cringe and run away, either.

We finally made it home. Fern was asleep, curled up in a ball on the front porch. "Look at her. Think she was worried about you?"

I sighed and smiled when Mom wasn't looking. I sat down next to her and stroked her hair, trying to wake her gently. She shot up and threw her arms around me, crying. "I'm sorry!"

"I'll be inside," Mom said softly.

I nodded. "Fern. What are you sorry for?"

"Didn't you get in trouble because of me?"

"No. I got in trouble for kicking Trevor Johnson in the face *after* you kicked his ass. I didn't like what he called you."

"I've been called worse. Don't ever get in trouble over that."

"I will. Each and every time someone calls you a nasty name. You don't deserve that."

"Okay. But then I get to punch everybody who calls *you* bad names."

"Um. No. It uh…doesn't work that way. You can actually kick people's asses. I can't. So, only I'm allowed to do stuff like that."

"Oh. Okay."

She had thrown her arms around me, but I finally lifted mine and wrapped them around her, hugging her back. Her breathing settled, and she was nice and warm in the cool air. "Would you like to come in?"

I could feel her nod, but she made no move to let go.

"Now?"

She shook her head. "I like this. Few more minutes."

I laughed. "I kind of like it, too."

Finally, she pulled back, but stopped just in front of my face, gazing into my eyes.

"What?"

"What you said earlier. Or didn't say, I should say. Is that how you feel?"

"Huh?"

"When Dean Smithandwesson said I was your girlfriend…"

"You mean Winchester," I said with a chuckle.

She nodded.

"You mean when I didn't say you weren't?"

She nodded again.

"Well. If you aren't opposed to the idea?"

She shook her head and bit her bottom lip.

"Lucy Fern, would you go out with me, defending me from the dangers of over-juiced jocks, snotty cheerleaders, and the possibility of attack by any feral polar bears that may or may not escape from the local zoo? To let me stare at your cute little butt in sickness and health? To have and to hold until the day you break up with me?"

"I do."

"I now pronounce us boyfriend and girlfriend."

Mom started clapping from the open front door. "I'm ordering pizza. What do you like on yours, Fern?"

"Meat."

"Meatlovers, it is. I assume that is okay with you, Mister Shakespeare?"

"Sounds good," I said, wanting to crawl into the bushes beside the front porch. Fern was a ninja. My mother was a ghost. Fire crept up my cheeks.

"Come inside. You two can have the couch tonight. I'll watch TV in my room. Cable is on."

I nearly shouted in excitement. Not for the cable. I could honestly care less. But with cable came great internet. "Sweet."

"Fern, Captain Reckless got suspended for two days. So you don't need to walk him to school tomorrow or Thursday," she said cryptically and headed into the kitchen to call in the order.

"You did?"

I nodded.

"I'll skip. I don't want to see those people. I might hurt them."

"No. Don't. You need an education..." I protested sarcastically.

"You want me to hurt them?" She sounded confused.

"I was kidding, Fern. I don't mind if you don't go. It's not like your grades will suffer."

"Can I spend time with you?"

"Of course. You're always welcome here." A tear fell down her cheek, and I wiped it off. "Don't cry."

"I'm not. That was windshield wiper fluid. My windshields were dirty."

"Uh, huh. Want to watch a movie?"

"Sure."

∞ ∞ ∞

"It's one in the morning, Dane. Why don't you make sure Fern gets home okay and then get your ass to bed."

I looked down next to me. Fern had fallen asleep sometime during the third movie. I chuckled. "Carry her home, you mean. She's passed out."

"I don't mind if she stays. As long as you promise to stay in your room, and she sleeps out here. Do I need to get my sleeping bag and park it in front of your door?"

"No, Mother. I shall behave."

"Good boy. I'm loading the shot gun just in case."

"You don't have one."

"Try me."

I gulped. I thought she'd been joking, but her tone made me wonder otherwise. "I'm going to put her in my bed. I'll sleep on the couch."

"You're such a gentleman..."

"You were testing me, weren't you?"

"Maybe."

I stood up and scooped Fern into my arms. She seemed even lighter than usual. I didn't struggle at all. "G'night, Mom."

"Say goodnight when you come back out. I'll be waiting. Just to make sure."

"Mom. I is a gentlemans."

"Uh huh." She sighed. "I guess I should quit worrying. You are almost eighteen."

"I like that you worry. But, you don't need to. She's asleep. We *just* started dating. It will be a while before you *do* need to worry."

"Okay. Night, Dane. Love you."

"Love you, too."

Mom headed into her room, and I headed to mine with a girl in my arms. Life had become surreal.

Fern reached up and wrapped her arm around my neck, rubbing her face against my chest. I turned sideways to get through the bedroom door. Laying her down gently, I lifted the comforter over her, hoping she wouldn't be uncomfortable in her jeans and hoodie. I wasn't at the point where I could exactly strip her, either. Turning to leave, she whispered, "Stay."

I sat down next to her and smiled. "I can't. I *will* be out in the living room if you need anything. If my mother saw me sleeping in here with you, she'd kill me."

She nodded. "Come back later then."

I chuckled and leaned over to kiss her forehead. "Good night, my Fern."

"You want to touch my butt?"

I lifted the comforter and poked the side of her butt. "Thanks. I'll sleep better now."

She smiled and closed her eyes. "Night, Dane."

"Night, Fern."

CHAPTER 8

I woke up struggling to breathe. I wasn't choking; something heavy was lying on my chest. Opening my eyes, all I saw was purple. I reached up and moved the handful of hair covering my eyes. My mom stood over me, scowling.

I begged for my life with only my eyes. She shook her head and ran her finger over her throat. "I put her into bed, I swear," I whispered.

She motioned at Fern. I glanced down over her hoodie. She had removed her pants sometime during the night and decided to fall asleep on top of me in her underwear. I sighed and whimpered a little. No wonder my mother was less than happy.

"She had pants on when I left her in my room last night. This isn't my fault, I swear."

She sighed and walked over to the recliner, grabbing the throw she kept there for napping. She opened it and tossed it over the two of us.

"I'm going to meet the mechanic at the car. He's going to see if he can get it started. Isn't she going to school?"

I shook my head. "She's skipping."

"I don't condone that behavior, either."

"She didn't want to run into the two of them without me…"

"Um. They're suspended, too."

"Oh. Yeah. I should have thought of that." I turned and smiled at the back of the purple head by my face. "That little minx. She tricked me."

Mom chuckled. "Behave while I'm gone. Seriously. Don't do anything stupid you'll regret later, please."

Mom left without another word.

I closed my eyes and fell back asleep for a little while. When I opened my eyes again, Fern was awake and watching me sleep, chin on her hands atop my chest. "Morning."

"Morning, Dane."

"You fell asleep on me again."

"I know."

"My mother saw you. Without pants."

"I know. I was awake."

"I um. Need to pee. Could you let me up?"

She slid forward a couple of inches and kept staring at me. "What?"

"Can I kiss you?"

I blinked in surprise. "Yeah, but you may want to wait until I brush my teeth. I'm just saying."

"No." She slid forward and lifted herself up. I glanced down and saw she wasn't wearing her normal white T-shirt. She wasn't wearing anything under the hoodie. She had unzipped it and used it as a blanket over the two of us while we slept. I gulped. She was absolutely beautiful and almost naked. It affected me. A fact that didn't go unnoticed by her. She giggled a little as she moved in closer, pressing her lips against mine.

I'd never really done more than one kiss on the lips in eighth grade. This was my first real open-mouthed, dancing-tongue kind of kiss. Fern groaned into my mouth. It was the single greatest event in my life. I wanted more. That would be a *huge* mistake, though. I gently lifted her up, breaking the kiss.

"Why did you stop?"

"Because that was perfect. Any more and um…"

"What?"

"I would want to do more than just kiss you."

"Oh. I'm okay with that."

"Fern. We just started dating a few hours ago. We are in no rush, whatsoever. Slow."

She sighed and plopped her head back down on my chest.

"That was really nice," I added. "That was my first kiss. I was expecting it to be awkward and semi-dangerous."

"That was your first?"

"You've kissed a guy before?" Not gonna lie. That kinda hurt.

"Not a guy."

"I need to pee. Please let me up."

"Okay."

I ran for the bathroom as fast as I could, picturing my grandmother in a bikini. That worked quickly. I used the bathroom and brushed my teeth, ready to face the world, or at least an amorous Fern. I found her still lying on the couch. She'd zipped up her hoodie but had yet to put on any pants.

Intent on brightening her morning, I slipped into the kitchen and made her a cup of coffee. Grabbing my morning Coke, I walked into the kitchen and offered the mug to her. She greeted it with a smile. I'm not joking, she said, "Good morning, coffee."

"Want me to turn on the TV?"

"If you want."

I needed some background noise. The living room was just too silent. I pressed the power button on the remote lying on the edge of the coffee table and sat back on the couch, not really caring what came on.

Fern set her half empty coffee mug on the table and lay down next to me, using my leg as a cushion. Her hoodie was covering most of her, thankfully. I reached down and stroked her hair.

The front door clicked and kicked open. Mom stood there, several bags of groceries in each hand and two dangling from her mouth.

"Mph mphhhh mph mphhhhh," she said exasperatedly.

I tried not to laugh, honestly. I did.

Sliding out from under Fern, I ran to the door and took the two out of her mouth and a bundle from one of her hands.

"Thank you."

"You're welcome. Two trips are for wussies, huh?"

"Yeah. And it's getting colder out."

"So, what was wrong with the car?"

She laughed. "Don't ask."

"Well, now you know I'm going to."

"In a rush to get to the school, I completely forgot to get gas."

"Oh. That's funny."

"The mechanic thought so, too. He got a real chuckle out of it. He was really nice about it, though. Gave me a can of gas and didn't charge me."

"He probably took one look at your car and figured you'd be a repeat customer anyway…"

"Good point. But at least we have food in the house."

I helped her put the groceries away. Fern ambled up and sat down at the counter, sipping her coffee and listening to our banter. I grabbed the pot off the maker and filled her cup.

"Thank you."

"Morning, Fern," Mom said, and gave her a smile.

"Morning, Mrs. Evans."

"Are you hungry?"

Fern nodded excitedly.

"Would you like some eggs?"

"Please."

"Dane?"

"Sure. Thanks."

The groceries were away, and I took the opportunity to sit on the other stool next to Fern. I glanced down to see if she had put pants on. She hadn't. Sighing, I tried not to stare.

Fern turned toward me while Mom bent down and rummaged through the cabinet for a fry pan. "You're staring," she whispered.

I leaned in and kissed her nose. "Of course, I am. You're not wearing pants."

"Should I put some on?"

I nodded.

"I hate pants."

"They're overrated. But, I value my life. If you don't put some on, my mom will blame me."

She nodded, sliding off the stool and heading back toward my bedroom. My mom, so far, had been pretty cool about things. Cooler than I'd ever have imagined. I didn't want to push my luck.

"Thank you," Mom said softly from the other side of the counter.

"You're welcome."

Fern returned, wearing her leggings and sat back down next to me. She picked up her coffee. "I have pants."

"I see that."

"But now you can't see my butt."

I shook my head and laughed. "It's getting warm in here. You can take off your hoodie if you'll be more comfortable."

She almost dropped her coffee. "I can't," she said and averted her eyes.

"Oh. You don't have a shirt on?"

She thought about it for a moment and nodded.

"You don't remember if you have a shirt on?"

She shrugged.

I let it go.

"Dane, make some toast."

Mom was busy stirring the eggs in the pan, making sure they didn't burn. I got up and grabbed the fresh loaf off the counter and popped a few slices in the toaster. "You having some, Mom?"

"I'll have one. I wasn't hungry, but the eggs smell good."

I popped a third piece in and pushed down the button before grabbing the tub of fake butter out of the fridge. I had just set it down when I saw Fern shudder. A strange look passed over her face when Mom's phone started ringing.

She reached over and snagged it out of her purse. "Ugh. It's your dad. Let me see what he wants. Put the eggs on some plates."

Mom hit the answer button. "What?"

I grabbed a large spoon out of the wooden holder by the stove and started scooping eggs out into three equal piles.

"Yes. This is her?"

The second I finished, the toast popped. I grabbed a butter knife out of the drawer, smeared butter on them, and cut them in half, diagonally.

"Yes. I understand. You do know we were divorced?"

Half-listening, I put the toast on the plates and set one in front of Fern. She gave me a sad look and took it gingerly. I left one by the stove for Mom and went back to my seat. "Could you hand me the salt and pepper?" They were on the counter on the other side of Fern.

She handed them to me but didn't start eating.

"You okay?"

She shrugged and stared down at her eggs and toast.

"What's wrong?" I shoveled a pile of eggs on the corner of my toast and bit it off. I hadn't realized how hungry I'd been.

"Thank you. Yes. I'll make some arrangements with work."

My ears picked up the tone in Mom's voice. I slowly set my fork down as she pulled the phone away from her ear and shut it off. I was about to ask her what was going on when her face crumpled in a look of pure horror. The tears slid down her cheeks as she set her phone down and practically ran around the counter, wrapping her arms around me.

"What?"

I could feel her shake as she cried in my shoulder.

"Mom? What is it?"

"Your… father."

"Dad?"

She nodded. Still not pulling away.

"What happened? Is he okay?"

She shook her head, refusing to let go. "He's dead. There was an accident at work."

"That's not funny, Mom."

She started sobbing harder. Fern's hand squeezed my arm. I stared at the pile of scrambled eggs on my plate for a moment before my vision turned black. I remember the sensation of falling, and Mom screaming my name.

CHAPTER 9

I came to in my own bed. Fern was nestled in the crook of my arm, her face against my chest. I was shocked I could feel her, being as numb as I was. It's amazing how fast life goes from okay to Shitsville in point-eight seconds.

I'd been unforgivably mad at the man, but he didn't deserve to die. Trying to picture never seeing him, or hearing his horrible laugh again, broke my heart.

Fern's warm hand cupped my cheek, turning my head toward hers. "I'm sorry about your dad."

"Thanks. Where's Mom?"

"Sleeping in her room. She wouldn't stop crying."

"She probably regrets everything we said to him before we moved. I know I do."

"You shouldn't. What he did was absolutely horrible. He deserved whatever words you had for him."

I opened my mouth to tell her she was wrong, but she wasn't. It's amazing how your respect of the dead includes forgiving their past sins almost instinctively. Instead of arguing, I kissed her forehead. "Sorry for passing out."

"It's okay. I protected you."

"You always do."

"Always will."

"Even years from now when you are finally tired of me?"

Her eyebrows lowered in confusion.

"Nothing. Never mind. Just not having a high self-esteem moment."

She buried her face in my neck and put her hand on my chest, her nail drawing a lazy circle. "I could never get tired of you. It's almost like I can't get enough of you."

"That's how all relationships start. It's probably one of the reasons I want to take thing so slow. I would hate to see you get bored too quick."

"Never. That is a useless worry."

She unzipped her hoodie and lay against my arm. I expected the feel of flesh on my arm, but she *did* have a shirt on underneath. She must have put it on after I passed out.

"You sure do love that hoodie, don't you?"

She nodded. "It's a part of who I am."

That was cryptic. "You're a member of the hoodie foundation? Knights of the hoodie?"

She lifted her head and smiled. "Something like that."

"Cool. Can I join?"

"You wouldn't want to. It's not for everybody. I was born into it. Molded by it…"

I laughed and kissed her nose. Then, the pain of loss came rushing back. I'm sure she noticed, because she began massaging my heart.

"Maybe I should check on Mom."

"I just did. Let her get some rest."

"So, what did I miss?"

"I caught you as you fell to the ground. Your mom was kind of hysterical. I brought you into your room and got you on your bed. She wanted to call an ambulance. Once I got you settled, I sat with her and calmed her down. She told me the whole story. I can let you know, or you can wait for her to tell you."

"Might as well get it out of the way. My dad was a lawyer. How the hell does someone die in an office?"

There. I said it. My dad was. *Not my dad* is. *Now it's real.*

"One of the clients, who your dad represented, didn't like having to pay lifetime alimony to his ex-wife… He showed up with a gun and shot your father."

"Jesus. Did they catch him?"

"He shot himself after."

"Good."

"I'm sorry, Dane."

"You didn't pull the trigger," I said and turned to face her, pulling her a little closer to me. "But, thank you. For caring."

She nodded. Not saying anything else. Then I felt the tiniest of kisses just above the collar of my T-shirt. It spoke to me more than any words of comfort ever could.

I tightened my arms around her just a little more.

"There is some good news, but I will let your mother share that with you."

"No way. I could use some good news right about now."

"Your mother will no longer be struggling as much financially. Your father had yet to remove her from his life insurance policy. She is the sole recipient of a large sum of money…"

I sighed, glad. Not that he had died. I was glad my mother would be taken care of. My father's biggest concern was how much the divorce was going to cost him. I'd heard him talking to one of his friends one night. It was one of the reasons I'd gone with my mom, that and the whole "I'm going to bang my secretary and move in with her" thing. He'd gotten off scott free except for child support. He made enough as a divorce attorney to be comfortable with that.

"Karma," I whispered.

"The three-fold law."

I gulped, not wanting to think about it, anymore. "I'm starving. Want to get some food?"

"May I use your shower first?"

"Sure. Do you need to run home and get some clean clothes?"

She sniffed herself and shook her head. "No. Can I borrow some of your deodorant?"

"You can borrow anything you need."

That made her smile. "Even your toothbrush?"

"Um. If you want to?"

"I do. My teeth feel funny." She sat up and looked down at me for a moment. "Will you be okay for a few minutes?"

"I'm fine, Fern. Thank you."

She bent down to give me another kiss before standing up and pulling her pants and panties off in one fluid motion. I could only imagine... Her hoodie still covered her, thankfully. "Fern!"

"What?"

I just shook my head. She smiled, turned around, and lifted the hoodie over one cheek. "Thought seeing my butt would cheer you up a little."

I couldn't help it. I laughed. She was right. "Towels are in the closet in the bathroom. Shampoo and stuff are on the shelf. Sorry. I only have manly-smelling body wash."

She headed into the bathroom. I heard the shower and the faucet turn on and smiled. My girlfriend was taking a shower at my house. With a grin plastered on my face, I put my hands under my head and stared up at the ceiling. It lasted for almost a minute before the tremendous weight of loss settled back in my chest.

I must have dozed off. I remember hearing someone walking in my room. Cracking open one eye. Fern stood at the end of my bed, towel hanging below the hoodie. She had wrapped it around her waist. The hoodie hung open, unzipped. I closed my eye, dozing in and out. My eye cracked open again, and she was staring at my face. She shrugged and turned back around, removing the towel.

She dropped the hoodie over her shoulders and began toweling her skin, working it underneath instead of taking it off. My sleep-addled brain didn't understand why. She pulled her arms out of the sleeves and the hoodie didn't fall down, it floated in the air behind her, like some sort of black mist.

I must be dreaming.

I blinked, and she was pushing an arm back through the sleeve. I knew I had been dreaming. Hoodies don't float. I closed my eyes again and rolled over on my side, facing the wall. I heard something fall to the ground. Without rolling back over, I turned my head and looked over my shoulder. Fern had knocked something off my dresser and bent over to pick it up. Luckily, she turned, or I would have had the view of a lifetime.

"You okay?"

"Yeah. Dropped your deodorant."

I rolled back over as she stood up. She raised her arm and finished spreading the gel stick, popping the cap back on it. She stopped to watch me, watching her. "I need to get dressed," she said, and made a spinning motion with her hand.

"Oh, now you're shy?" I wasn't complaining, merely teasing her.

"I um… I need to take my hoodie off to put my T-shirt on."

"And that embarrasses you?" I was being sincere. I kind of wanted to know why she *never* took it off. I assumed she had, to go in the shower since it wasn't sopping wet, but I was starting to wonder if I would ever see this particular phenomenon.

She didn't say anything, just nodded shyly.

Poor body image? Low self-esteem?

Either way, it kind of broke my heart. I slid to the end of the bed and crooked a finger at her. She zipped up her hoodie and stepped closer, but not close enough to touch.

"You know I think you are absolutely beautiful, don't you?"

"You just like my butt."

I laughed a little, glad to see her joking. "Fern. I like *all* of you. Your purple hair, your soft smile, your adorable face. I like the way you watch me when I watch you. I love the way you smell, kind of like flowers and now Old Spice. I love the sound of your voice and how strange you can be at times. I love how you protect me and comfort me. I even love your over-sized black hoodie."

"What about my butt?"

"Love that, too."

"What if part of me was horrendously ugly?"

"It wouldn't matter. You would still be you, and you would still be beautiful."

She sighed and lowered her eyes. I knew there was something she wanted to tell me, but was worried. I would never force her or even ask her to show me.

"Is there something you are afraid to tell me or show me?"

She nodded, not taking her eyes off the floor.

"Well, guess what?"

"What?"

"I can tell you right now, it doesn't matter to me. If you want to keep it hidden until you're comfortable enough to show me, I don't mind. I'll turn around so you can put your shirt on. There's T-shirts in the middle two drawers if you want to borrow one," I said, and flipped over onto my stomach, burying my head under the pillows.

The dresser drawer opened and closed; I could hear that much. There was also the sound of her unzipping her hoodie. I fought the temptation to look. She probably wouldn't have been mad, but I know she would have been hurt. There was no way I could do that.

She tapped my leg.

"Is it safe?"

"Turn around."

I pulled the pillows off my head and turned around. She was wearing my T-shirt and nothing else. She didn't need to. It looked almost like a dress on her. Her hair was a frizzy mess, and her cheeks were flushed from embarrassment. She'd never looked more beautiful. For the life of me, I couldn't figure out what she'd been worried about.

"You look beautiful…"

She smiled, but looked sad and shook her head. She turned around, and I saw the lumps on her back, even through the T-shirt. Up by her shoulders were the largest two, side by side. From there, fanning down were multiple ridges crisscrossing all the way down to her waist. I'd been expecting something, much, much, worse.

"Does it hurt?"

"No. Not at all."

I could understand why she wore the hoodie to school. If anybody had an inkling… It would not have been easy for her. I didn't blame her for never wanting to take it off. But they were not me. I hadn't been lying about what I told her. I stood up and crossed the distance between us. She spun around and started backing away in a panic. When she backed into the wall, I wrapped my arms around her and held her tight.

"Yep. Still beautiful."

She melted into my embrace and threw her arms around me, hugging me tight. She nearly broke my spine. "Um… Fern… You're breaking me."

"Oh! Sorry," she said, and loosened her grip.

I kissed the top of her head.

CHAPTER 10

"Are you ready to go?"

I nodded at my mother, but I wasn't. Not really.

"We'll be back this weekend," she reminded me softly.

"I know." She didn't understand. I was sad to be leaving Fern for a few days, but the real reason I wasn't ready to go was because I wasn't ready to put my father in the ground. I didn't think I'd ever be. Not with the way I left things between us. And now I'd never have a chance to forgive him.

Fern squeezed my hand. I think she knew why I didn't want to go. Sometimes I swear she could read my mind.

"I'll miss you," I whispered in her ear.

"I know. I'll send you pictures of my butt."

"Make sure you have pants on."

"No promises. I'm sorry you have to do this alone."

"I won't be. I'll have Mom, and she'll have me. We'll get through this."

"I know you will."

I leaned over and kissed her, giving her hand one final squeeze before letting it go. I left her standing on my front porch as I made a mad dash through the rain for the car waiting to take us to the airport. She waved the entire time it took us to load up, back up, and drive away.

"You're not going to go into withdrawals, are you?"

I shook my head at my mother in the back seat with me. "It's not Fern, Mom. I'm just depressed. This would be easier

83

if the last time I talked to him, I didn't tell him he was a piece of shit. That, and I never wanted to see him again."

"That's nicer than my last words to him."

"Now, I can't ever take it back."

"He knows. Death really isn't the end. Or, at least I hope it's not. When I'm gone, I really want to haunt you and keep you out of trouble. Somebody's gotta watch you, and Fern is worse than you are."

I chuckled. She wasn't wrong there.

"At least you got her to keep her pants on more often."

The driver of the car shot me a look in the rearview mirror...

"Yeah, cuz wearing shorts in Virginia in the fall is just crazy..."

I elbowed my mother.

She snorted and looked out the window. "I didn't think I'd be going back to Chicago this soon."

"At least we get to see Gramma and Grampa."

"Yeah. Yay."

"Oh, stop. They're sweet."

"To you. You're their grandchild. Know how many times Grampa has said 'I told you so' since I left your father?"

"I can imagine."

"No. You really can't. Thank God the man doesn't know how to text. The number would have tripled, easily."

My phone happened to *ding* in my pocket. I pulled it out and opened the picture text from Fern. It was her ass. At least she had pants on. I started laughing.

Mom looked over at my phone and sighed. "There is something wrong with that girl."

"Just figuring that out?"

"No. I knew from the start. But she really can be sweet. You and she were made for each other. I hate to admit it."

"So, does this mean I have your blessing to marry her?"

Mom's eyes went wide, and she started sputtering.

"In ten years or so," I added with a wink.

"You're a little shit."

"Nope. I'm a big shit now."

It took us almost an hour to get to the airport, another hour to get through security, and an hour to get on the damn plane. We could have driven to Chicago faster. If Mom's car would have made the trip. She wasn't so sure and didn't want to risk it. Even if it meant Grampa was picking us up at the airport.

When we got off the plane, he was standing there in the row of drivers, holding up a sign that had our last names on it. He even had one of those flat gray hats chauffer drivers wore.

"That man has too much free time," Mom whispered when she saw him.

I laughed.

"Hey, Grampa," I said when we were close enough.

"Master Dane, your ride awaits," he said with a bow and a laugh.

"Hi, Daddy."

"Hi, Connie Bug."

I couldn't help but snicker. He always called her that. No matter where or when, Mom was his Connie Bug.

Then Grampa got serious. "Are you two doing okay?"

We nodded in unison, solemnly.

He hugged us both.

"Come on. Gramma's circling the airport. Let's get outside before she makes another go."

"Still too cheap to pay for parking, Dad?"

"Bet your ass. Ten dollars an hour. Robbery."

At least Mom and I didn't have to pick up any luggage. We just had our carry-on bags. "Three days does not necessitate luggage," she had told me. I don't think she realized it, but she was turning into Grampa.

We stood out on the curb of the airport, waiting for Gramma to come back around. My phone finally picked service back up and went off in my pocket again. I pulled it out, made sure the old people were still talking and checked my messages.

Miss you already.

Miss you more, I replied. *Just landed. Let you know when we get to the Grandparents.*

Ok

I slipped my phone into my pocket.

"Who was that, your girlfriend?" Grampa had stopped talking and was watching me.

"Yeah," I replied, and took great enjoyment at watching his face twist in surprise.

"You have a girlfriend?"

"Yep."

"Show me a picture."

"I only have pictures of her butt on my phone…"

Mom reached over and slapped me in the back of the head.

"Let me see," Grampa said with even more excitement.

A sigh and a slap later, and Grampa was rubbing the back of his head, too. "Worth it," he whispered.

∞ ∞ ∞

Nothing ever seemed more final in my entire life as watching my father's casket being lowered slowly into the ground. I walked up and picked a rose from the pile and gently tossed it in, feeling its impact in my heart.

I'd spent the entire day in a daze. I vaguely remembered the funeral and mildly recollected getting up to say a few words. If anyone asked me what I had said, I wouldn't have been able to tell them.

The only thing that clearly stood out was Dad's girlfriend trying to start a scene with Mom. Nobody let it happen. Dad's brother and his wife swooped down on the woman like a pair of eagles fighting over a rabbit. She was out the door before Mom even had to defend herself. I needed to thank Uncle Joe before we left.

A hand on my shoulder broke me from my reverie. There were people behind me waiting to pay their respects, too. "Sorry," I said blindly to whoever tried to comfort me and stumbled off to the side, not stopping until I found some trees out of view of the gaping hole in the ground.

My phone buzzed in my pocket.

I'm with you. <3

The tears started flowing down my face. I smiled at my phone before a drop fell on my screen, warping her message in the middle.

I know. Thank you. That was hard.

You'll be home tomorrow, and this will all be a bad memory.

What doesn't kill us makes us stronger, I replied.

The people you love make you stronger.

My fingers paused over the keys. Blame the situation, blame my broken heart for making me sentimental. For the rest of my life, I would always tell people how I felt while I had the chance. While I had it. *Then* you *make me stronger.*

It took a few minutes for her to respond. I could almost picture her staring at her phone to make sure I was saying what she thought I was saying. She took long enough to respond that *I* was starting to panic. Maybe I *shouldn't* have told her how I felt…

Did you just tell me that you love me?

Or she could have just been confused. *Yes… Is that okay?*

YES

Then I'll say it again the right way. Fern, I love you.

87

I like you, too.

What?

Just kidding. I love you, too.

And just like that, the day was a little brighter. The hole in my heart had filled a little. I put my phone back in my pocket and took a deep breath. It was cold outside. Way colder than Virginia. I could see my breath fog, even in the sunlight. For the first time in my life, I was grateful to be wearing a suit jacket.

"You okay?"

Mom had come up next to me without me even noticing. "I'll live. You okay?"

She nodded, not elaborating.

"Where's the bitch?" I didn't need to clarify who I was talking about. We'd been calling her that all day.

"Crying in the front row. I think everybody is tired of her shit."

"I know Uncle Joe is. That was cool the way he and Aunt Suzy played defense for you."

"Joe wanted to beat the shit out of your dad when he found out what was going on, so I'm not surprised. He was always the smart one of the family."

It was my turn to nod.

"Bitch said something about suing for her share of the insurance money. Joe told her where to go, right there in front of everybody. It got really awkward, so I figured I'd find my prodigal son."

"I just needed some time. I talked to Fern, too."

"How is she?"

I shrugged. "She hasn't said. She was texting to comfort me."

"You should ask. It will make her smile."

"I told her I love her."

"Or you could do that. You sure?"

"I am. I'd be a fool not to."

"Well, you are a fool, but not about this. I wish you both many years of happiness. I hope you turn into that happy, old couple who started dating in high school."

"And I'll stay away from secretaries…"

"That's an even better plan. Can I be honest?"

"I should hope so."

"I think your dad didn't leave us because he didn't love us. I think he did it to feel younger. Mid-life crisis sort of thing. Maybe by banging a twenty-two-year-old, he could recapture some of his youth."

"You did say Uncle Joe was the bright one of the family."

"I'm glad you see how stupid that was."

"Love is love. Beauty is on the inside. Know why Fern always wears that hoodie?"

"I thought it was a fashion statement."

"No. Her back is disfigured. That's why she never takes it off. It hides the lumps and ridges."

"How did you find out?"

"I told her before she showed me that there wasn't a single inch on her that I wouldn't find beautiful. She took the hoodie off and showed me. Even through a T-shirt, it was obvious."

"I hope you didn't react badly…"

"I hugged her and told her she was beautiful."

"How did I raise such a good kid?"

"One that gets suspended from school for fighting?"

"For the right reasons. So yes."

"Just had a good teacher," I said, and hugged my mother one more time before we headed back to the grave.

"Love you, Dane."

"Love you too, Ma."

CHAPTER 11

It was almost midnight when the van pulled up to the house. Mom had prepaid for the ride back from the airport, but she handed him a nice tip. "Do you need help getting your things?"

"No. We just have the two little bags."

I pulled the handle on the side door and it slid back, letting the cool night air into the van. We got out and trudged up the sidewalk, exhausted. It had been a long day.

I half expected Fern to be sitting on the porch, but she wasn't there, even though I'd texted her when we landed. She had never responded. I'd assumed she had either fallen asleep or was planning a surprise. I guessed the former won out.

Mom opened the door and let me in first. I wheeled the suitcase up the last step and into the house, heading for bed. "It's *really* late. You can stay home tomorrow if you want. I'll write you a note for school."

"Are you going to work?"

"Yeah. I gotta. I don't want to, but I have to. The old manager is retiring this Friday. I have a week to learn the ins and outs of the store."

"You'll do great. I'll go to school tomorrow. I've already missed a week."

"Okay. Don't complain to me when you get up in the morning."

"Can I change my mind in the morning?"

She laughed. "This isn't a negotiation. If you need to stay home tomorrow, stay home."

"Thanks, Mom. Night."

"Night." She kissed me on my forehead and trudged to her room, closing the door behind her.

I headed for my room. My door was open, and the lights were off. I flicked the switch and almost screamed when Fern smiled at me from my bed.

"Hi, sailor."

I chuckled and shut the door behind me. "How did you get in?"

"Your Mom gave me a key to keep an eye on things and go through your underwear drawer when you weren't looking. I threw out all the tighty-whiteys. You look better in boxers."

"So, do I get to go through your underwear drawer?"

"Sure. Fair is fair. Oh. I love fairs. We should go."

I just laughed and set my suitcase by my dresser. Shucking my shoes and my pants, I lifted the cover and slid into my bed next to her. She immediately curled up into my arms.

"Do I want to know what you're wearing?"

"The usual."

I groaned. "That's what I was afraid of."

"Shut up and touch my butt. It missed you. So did I."

I stuck my arm under the cover and put it on her leg, sliding it up slowly over the mound of her cheek. I panicked when I didn't feel any panties until I slid it over her lower back and found the top of her thong. "Whew."

"Thought I was commando?"

I nodded.

"I thought about it, but the odds of me touching myself while waiting for you went up exponentially. So, I kept them on."

92

"I didn't need to know that."

"Why?"

"Because that's all I can picture in my head."

"Get some sleep. I'll show you tomorrow if you want…"

"Fern! If you don't stop, I'm not going to be *able* to sleep."

"Sure you will, just be careful rolling over on your stomach. Ouch."

I shook my head. The girl had zero filter. But as she lay there in my arms, I was grateful to not be alone.

"I missed you," she whispered softly as she was dozing off.

"I missed you more."

∞ ∞ ∞

"Dane are you going to school?"

I looked over at my mother standing in the doorway and staring at Fern still sleeping in my arms.

"Yeah. Since I'm awake."

"Okay. Guess she missed you."

"Yep," I said, and rolled over onto my back, too tired to open my eyes. "Good luck at work today."

"Don't get suspended today."

"Deal."

"Love you."

"Love you, too, Mom."

She shut the door behind her, and I rolled back over, kissing Fern's forehead. She opened her eyes and smiled sweetly. "Morning."

"Morning. Come on, it's time to go to school."

"Don't wanna."

"Me neither, but we have to. Did you go at all while I was gone?"

"No? Why would I, if you're not there?"

"You went before you met me, didn't you?"

"Sometimes. When I got bored sitting at home, and when I would get banned from the mall."

"You got banned from the mall?"

She nodded. "Four times."

"For what?"

"Once for a small fire in the Santa's village. Once for forgetting to pay for a gold necklace. Once for stopping a robbery. And once for forgetting to wear pants."

I wasn't surprised by any of them except for the robbery part. "Why did you get banned for stopping a robbery?"

"I destroyed the mannequin I used to beat him with."

Okay, that didn't surprise me either. "How do you get banned more than once?"

"I changed my hair color."

"Okay then. Wait, you haven't always had purple hair?"

"No. It was green two weeks ago."

"Huh. I like the purple. Don't get banned from the mall again."

"No promises."

She nuzzled in closer to my neck, and I breathed in her scent. She smelled like my body wash. "Were you using my shower while I was gone?"

She nodded.

"Is everything okay at your house?"

Again, she nodded. "I just like using your things."

"Sorry I took my toothbrush."

"That's okay. I put mine in your bathroom…"

"You moving in?"

She shook her head. "It's just dark and lonely at my house."

"Why don't you turn on a light?"

"They're broken."

I had a bad feeling in my stomach. "The bulbs?"

"Everything."

"Would you show me?"

"No."

"Why?"

"I don't want you to see."

"Fern. Take me to your house, please."

She sighed and got out from underneath the warm covers. "Okay." She didn't look happy about it, though. Almost afraid.

"We need to hurry and get to school, too."

She was wearing a black thong and didn't even make a look at my butt joke. There was something definitely wrong. I got up and grabbed my toothbrush out of my bag and a clean pair of pants and T-shirt. By the time I finished getting dressed and cleaned up, she was sitting on my couch, rocking back and forth.

"Ready?"

She shook her head.

"Come on, Fern." I pointed at the door. She actually dragged her feet as she walked.

We headed out the front door, and I followed behind her, watching her expression darken. We passed the neighbor's and walked up to a house that had seen better days. Our lawn had stopped growing and started browning. Fern's lawn looked like a wheat field, ready to be harvested. I made a mental note to come do it after school.

She opened the front door without unlocking it. I stepped into the set of a horror movie. The couch had been flipped over on its back, a gaping hole had been punched through the television, and the one painting hanging on the wall had been ripped and sat on a forty-five-degree angle. The rest of the walls had diagrams and symbols I had no chance of recognizing, thickly painted on the wall. It had dripped down, giving the appearance of running blood.

"Did you do this?" I asked her outright.

"No. Mother."

"Your aunt didn't clean it up?"

"She left."

I stepped over torn paper and broken glass, glancing into the kitchen. It was clean, dishes were stacked neatly in the sink. Three bento boxes sat on the counter.

"Want to change before school? Can I see your room?"

She nodded, leading me back through a dark hallway. I flipped the light switch, but nothing happened. Even Fern's room was dark, but tidy. It was just a little spartan. She literally had a bed and dresser. No desk, no nightstand. She opened her closet, and she had a few shirts hanging in there. No leftover toys from her childhood, keepsakes, artwork. Nothing to show she had ever grown up in the house. My heart ached for her.

She pulled off her hoodie but left her T-shirt on. Her misshapen back began to make a little more sense. Maybe her mother had beaten her. She turned around and made a shooing motion with her hand. She didn't want me to see her without her T-shirt. I nodded in understanding and walked back out into the hall, closing her door behind me.

The doorway across the hall had been left cracked open. I pushed it open a little more to see inside. Red paint covered the walls in unusual shapes and patterns, like in the living room. It covered the carpeted floor. I recognized one thing in the entire jumbled mess, a pentagram painted on the ceiling. Candles had been burned on every conceivable surface. The bed had been shredded. It looked like someone had run a lawnmower over it, repeatedly.

The layout of the house was almost identical to ours. I crossed to the other side of the house, wanting to see her mother's room. I had my hand on the knob when Fern called out from the living room. "Please don't."

"Fern. Forget school. Go pack your clothes. You are moving into my house. I'll talk to Mom tonight. She might set up the spare bedroom for you and litter the hall with booby traps, but she'll say yes."

Tears were running down her cheeks. I let go of the doorknob and ran to her, holding her and rubbing her back. It took nearly ten minutes before she stopped crying.

"Now you know why I didn't want you to see. I hate this place."

"Let's grab your stuff. We'll go to school tomorrow. Deal?"

She nodded, still sniffling. "Deal."

"Can you grab the bento boxes out of the kitchen and take them to your house? I'll get my clothes and meet you there. I… I need a few minutes."

"You sure?"

"Yes. Please."

I didn't want to leave her alone, but acquiesced. "Okay. Show me which ones to take."

She walked into the kitchen and picked out a couple. "Here. I can always come back for the others later."

I took them from her and brought them back to the house. Then pulled out my phone and texted my mother to give her a heads up.

Not going to school. Mom. I went to Fern's house… It's bad. I'm moving her into the spare room at our house, if that's okay. I'll fill you in later. Don't freak.

She didn't respond right away, but I kept glancing down at my phone, waiting for the eventual freak out. It was hard to tell with my mother. If I told her my girlfriend wanted to move in, she'd probably beat me to death with a shoe. If I said my girlfriend *needed* to move in because of a family situation, she'd probably adopt her. But that would make her my sister, and that would be gross.

I just wanted to make sure she was okay with it as soon as possible.

When the phone *finally* went off, I closed my eyes and took a deep breath before looking at the screen.

Is it really that bad, or are you being dramatic?

It's worse that you can imagine, I sent back.

Fine. But there's going to be rules. Guest *room! Not* your *room! Talk about it later. Love you.*

Love you, too.

CHAPTER 12

Mom hadn't been kidding when she said we would talk about it later, and it wasn't just me. She brought home Italian take-out and we sat at the dining room table, ate, and got lectured about the finer intricacies of having two seventeen-year-olds with hormones living under the same roof. I wanted to die.

She even firmly told Fern that under no circumstances was she to sleep in my room again. And to wear some damn pants. Fern looked confused but agreed anyway.

Mom put the blow-up air mattress in the spare room and built Fern a nest out of spare blankets and pillows. Fern seemed happy about it. We were going to the thrift store in town over the weekend and see about getting her some real furniture. I don't think Fern cared either way. Even with an inflatable mattress, the room at our house seemed cozier than her last one.

Surprisingly enough, I woke up alone in my own bed. She had actually listened.

Mom opened my door without knocking.

"Morning, sunshine. I'm heading to work."

"Have fun," I said, and groaned, not wanting to get out of bed.

"I made sure Fern is up. And made sure she slept in her room."

I lifted myself up on my elbow. I had thanked Mom for what she was doing, but sometimes, once isn't enough. "Thanks again for letting her stay."

She nodded but still looked overly concerned. Maybe I should have softened the picture I painted of Fern's house. "I'm still debating calling the police on that aunt of hers. Sure, Fern is seventeen, but last time I checked, that wasn't an adult capable of living on their own."

"I know. I'd be screwed if you ever ended up in the loony bin. The washing machine still scares me."

"Don't feel bad. Most men are hopeless creatures."

She smiled and ducked out of my room, letting me get ready. After five minutes more of sleep… I lay back on my pillow and closed my eyes. My door opened again. "I'm up!"

I sat up expecting my mother, but it was Fern. She padded softly into my room, wearing a T-shirt, hoodie, and socks. She looked like she hadn't slept in a week. Without a word, she crawled up into bed with me and lay on top of me. At least she was on top of the comforter.

"Oomph!"

She wasn't gentle when she plopped down, planting her head on my chest.

"Stay home?"

"We can't," I answered.

"Don't feel good."

"Look at me."

She lifted her head, slowly. It was the first time I'd ever gotten to take someone's temperature with the proven Mom method… I gently pressed my lips to her forehead and pulled back quickly. She had a fever. A bad one. She was practically burning up.

"Shit, Fern. Let me up. Lie on your back."

She rolled over, and I jumped out of bed, running to the kitchen and flinging open the cabinet where Mom kept the medicine. I grabbed a couple of ibuprofen and a glass of water. By the time I made it back to the bedroom, she had fallen back asleep. I shook her arm gently, and she opened her eyes.

"Here, baby. Take these."

She smiled and opened her mouth. I put the pills in, and she kissed the tip of my finger. Knowing there wasn't a chance in hell of not spilling water everywhere, I handed her the glass. She gulped down the entire thing and plopped her head back on the pillow.

"You can sleep in here if you want. If I don't get to school, Mom will give birth to a flock of canaries. Text me how you're doing. If I don't hear from you by lunch, I'll sneak out."

She nodded, sighing. I slid the cover out from underneath her and wrapped her up. "Thank you."

"I just hope you feel better quick. Let me know if you need anything. There's canned soup in the cabinet."

"Okay."

I watched her for a moment before getting up to get ready. It only took me a couple of minutes. I checked on Fern one last time before heading to school.

∞ ∞ ∞

My day ended up being miserable. It was a mix of sympathy for the loss of my father, and being ostracized even further for getting Trevor suspended for two weeks. I dealt with both the same way, I ignored it all. Ignored it, kept my head down, and concentrated on getting caught up on the week's worth of school I missed. Unfortunately, I missed a World History test on one of the days I was suspended. The teacher wouldn't let me take a make-up test, so that would end up being a zero averaged into my grade. The joys of high school.

By the time lunch rolled around, I hadn't heard from Fern. I bit the bullet, grabbed the school lunch, said a silent prayer before sitting down to eat, and texted my girlfriend to check on her.

You doing okay? If you're still sleeping, I'm sorry for texting.

I nibbled on the hamburger and played on the phone, waiting for her to text back. I made it halfway through the processed "meat" on the stale bun before she finally did.

Alive.

You need me to come home?

No. Soup and back to bed. I hurt.

I'll be home soon.

Okay. <3

<3

I closed my screen and chowed down on the rest of the "food" on my tray. Valerie and the rest of the cheerleaders were walking by me. Valerie said, with no effort whatsoever to be quiet about it, "His dad probably didn't die of natural causes, he probably killed himself out of embarrassment."

I knew they were talking about me. Glancing up, she flashed me a wicked smile to make sure I heard her. I just smiled back. "Yeah. He was upset I didn't get suspended for two weeks. I mean two days? That's like a slap on the wrist for kicking your dumb-shit boyfriend in the face."

The stunned looks on their faces made it totally worth it. I was probably going to get my ass beat, but I found myself not caring. I'd had my ass kicked by scarier people than her jock-strap boyfriend.

The silence in the cafeteria was deafening as I picked up my tray and walked away.

"Screw you and your whore freak of a girlfriend!"

"No thanks. We're happy by ourselves. Not really into threesomes with skank cheerleaders," I called over my shoulder. Several people clapped as I walked out the door.

I skipped the rest of lunch and slowly walked to my next class, aimlessly wandering the halls on the way.

By the time the last bell of the day rang, I had a mountain of homework and no will to live. Typical day of high school. However, being the nice individual that I was, I also collected all of Fern's missing assignments and homework. She could be miserable with me. At least it would give her something to do while I did mine.

I practically ran out the exit, pulling my jacket a little tighter around me. I made it about halfway home when I noticed the gray Mustang following me slowly. I turned just as they were passing me in time to see Trevor Johnson fling a beer bottle from the passenger window. It was a perfect throw that I didn't have a chance of dodging. I felt the impact on my forehead, heard the sound of crunching bone. The feel of blood flowing down my face was the last thing I remember.

∞ ∞ ∞

"Are you okay?"

"What the hell happened?" I looked over at the nurse in blue surgical scrubs holding a clipboard and checking the machines monitoring me.

"Somebody launched a beer bottle at your head. You had multiple lacerations and a nice concussion. You should be fine. Look at the bright side, chicks dig scars."

"How bad?"

"Doc did a nice job with the stitches. Shouldn't be *too* bad. Your eyebrow might be split in the middle forever, though. Your cheek probably won't even be noticeable. You see who did it?"

I shook my head. I thought I saw Trevor throw it, but I wasn't a hundred percent sure. The bitch Valerie must have texted him the minute I walked out of the lunchroom. "No. Just saw a gray Mustang."

"Well, there's a nice police officer outside waiting to take a report. I'll let him know you're up. Your mother was here, but she went home to check on someone?"

"Fern. My…uh…my girlfriend. She's sick at home."

"She lives with you?"

"Long story, but different rooms."

"I'm one of those non-judgey nurses. Kudos, kiddo. Need some condoms?"

My eyes widened in shock. Which was stupid on my part. "Ow, ow, ow." I grabbed my eyebrow and forehead.

"My bad," the nurse said, and walked out of the room.

A bored-looking cop walked in. The nurse was prettier.

"Dane Evans?"

"In the newly stitched flesh."

"Want to tell me what happened?"

"There's not much to tell. Left school, was walking home when some asshole threw a beer bottle out of a car window at me. Hit me in the face."

"I see that. Did you see who did it?"

"No. Just saw them riding in a gray Mustang. No, I didn't get the plate. All I could see was Budweiser and blood."

"Well. If you see the car again, dial 911. We have most of the beer bottle, but the odds of getting prints off that…"

"Yeah. I figured."

"If you think of anything else, give me a call." He handed me an Oak Hills Police Department business card with his name on it.

"Thanks, Detective James."

"Feel better, kid."

He walked out, and I closed my eyes. Surprisingly, I wasn't in a lot of pain, but resting my eyes felt really good. The throbbing in my head played a nice, soft rhythm.

104

My mother was sitting next to my bed when I opened my eyes an hour later. "Hey, Mom."

"Was it that kid again?"

"Good to see you, too. How was your day?"

She stood up and walked over to the bed. "Sorry, sweetie. Just a little pissed off right now."

"Yeah. Me, too. To answer your question…probably. I don't know. How is Fern?"

"Sleeping. You're lucky I saw your texts to her and knew to check on her. Next time, let me know."

"Sorry. Didn't think of it. Found out she was sick after you left."

"Well, now you know for next time."

"Yeah."

"You ready to go home?"

"I don't have to stay?"

"This is the emergency room. They fix you and you leave, but they said you could rest for a while."

"Hell yes, I want to go home." My shirt was crinkly from all the blood. Gross.

"Come on. You're excused from school for a few days. The principal will be working with the detective and giving him a list of all the students with gray Mustangs."

"I'm surprised. It didn't happen on school property, and Trevor is suspended until next week."

"Well, hopefully this gets his ass thrown out."

CHAPTER 13

Fern's face when she saw mine, broke my heart. It was the lip quiver that did it. "What happened?"

I gave her the rundown, and her face darkened with every word. She looked like she was going to strangle Trevor, even if it *wasn't* him that threw the bottle.

"I want you to promise me you won't go after him."

"No."

"Fern."

She rolled over, turning her back to me. "No."

"Fern, this needs to end. You retaliate, he retaliates. It's because I didn't keep my mouth shut at lunch today that this–"

"What happened at lunch?" She rolled back over and stared at me, obviously in pain. She was straining to move.

"Are you okay? Need some more ibuprofen?"

"Dane. *What happened at lunch*?"

"Valerie being Valerie."

"What did she *do*?"

"She didn't do anything. She just was mouthing off and said something mean."

I could tell she didn't believe me. So, I reluctantly told her the whole story. I didn't leave anything out. Instead of angry, she looked heartbroken. She tried to reach up to touch my face, but I could see her shaking from the effort. I lowered my face to her.

She cupped my cheek and tried to ignore the stitches on my face; her eyes darted to the wound. "It doesn't hurt that bad. Do you dig scars?"

"Not on you. I was supposed to protect you."

"Yeah. But I was busy taking care of you. Get better, and then you can get back on the job."

She nodded. "I'm tired, I'll go back to my room."

"No. I am. I already told Mom. You want me to ask her if I can stay in here with you tonight?"

"No. I don't want to get you sick. Ask her when I feel better."

"That's not how that works."

"Then I'll just sneak in here once I feel better. You sure you don't want your bed?"

"I'm sure." I tucked the blanket around her a little tighter. "Need anything else?"

"A kiss."

"I suppose I could do *that*." I leaned over and gently kissed her lips. She felt a hundred degrees cooler than she had that morning. "You aren't running as bad of a fever as you were."

"I feel better, just hurt all over."

"Get some sleep. Hopefully you feel better in the morning. Wake me up if I'm not up."

"Okay," she said, and closed her eyes, bundled up in my bed. I smiled and kissed her again, gently on the forehead.

"Night, Fern."

"Night."

∞ ∞ ∞

I woke up to searing pain in my head. Apparently, the pain killers had worn off. I rolled over to get out of bed, and was unceremoniously dumped onto the floor by the air mattress I had forgotten I was sleeping on. "Ouch."

I got up and walked into the kitchen to grab some more pills out of the small bottle Mom had laid out for me with a note with explicit instructions to take two pills only. Exclamation point, exclamation point, exclamation point. So not only was my mother worried I would be sinning with my girlfriend, but turning to a life of becoming addicted to prescription pain-killers.

"Thanks, Mom," I whispered, and popped two of them in my mouth as I walked over to the fridge to take a swig right out of the orange juice container.

I looked at the clock. It was almost eight in the morning, and Mom had left for work. I decided to check on Fern and headed for my room. Without knocking, I opened the door. She was lying on her back with the covers kicked off her. Not wanting to wake her up, I crossed the room silently and bent over her with the sole intention of checking her temperature.

Her hair was damp, and she smelled like body wash. She must have gotten up in the middle of the night and taken a shower. I didn't blame her; she was sweating pretty bad yesterday. I lowered my lips to her forehead, and her eyes popped open.

My lips pressed against her, and she felt *almost* warm, which was pretty normal for her. "Feeling better?"

She nodded. "I felt so gross, I had to take a shower. How are you feeling?"

"Pretty shitty, but I just took some medicine. So hopefully that will help."

"Lay down."

I didn't argue. I felt like I was going to fall over anyway. I sighed as I landed and curled up next to her for a change, resting my head on her chest. "You're pretty comfortable."

"Sorry my boobs aren't bigger."

"Shush. Perfect."

"Me or my boobs?"

"All three of you."

She giggled, and my head bounced. So much for the happiest place on earth. Even my eyeballs hurt. "Sorry!"

"It's okay. Didn't want to get rid of that concussion, anyway."

"I'm sorry, Dane," she said apologetically.

"Don't worry about it. It was my fault."

She propped a pillow under my head and gently crawled on top of me, staring at me the whole time. She spread her legs and straddled my waist. I tried *very* hard to ignore the fact she was not wearing any pants under her overly long hoodie. A fact that had become quite apparent. I focused on her eyes.

She put her hands on the bed just under my arms and lowered her face to mine. "I want to make it up to you," she purred into my ear before running her tongue over it.

A shiver wiggled its way down my spine. "Um. How?"

She trailed her lips along my jaw and gently kissed my cheek. "Something like this."

"This is good."

"You like this?"

I could only nod as she licked my lower lip. It felt like the temperature had gone up in my room by about fifty-thousand degrees. She slid down a little lower than my waist and lifted up my shirt.

"Fern..."

"Don't say a word. Every word you say, I go a step further..."

I wisely chose to remain silent. I trusted her to stop before we went *too* far. Mostly. Kind of maybe.

Her tongue ran along my collarbone, and then she grazed my shoulder with her teeth. She gave a little growl as she tasted my skin. I shuddered beneath her. I wondered what I should do with my hands and settled with putting them on her hips. She lifted herself off me for a moment and pulled her sweatshirt out from underneath her. Leaning in, she pressed her lips against mine and reached back with one hand, pulling my hand from her waist and sliding it over her butt. She wore normal panties and not a thong, thank God. They still felt silky smooth under my hands, and I gripped her tight, my other hand following the lead.

She groaned as we kissed, and I kneaded her flesh. Her mouth opened, and her tongue darted in my mouth. It was my turn to moan. I'd had champagne a few times in my life. That bubbly sweetness is the only thing I could compare the taste and feel of her lips to. And then she began to dance with her hips.

I didn't know what to do as she rubbed against me. I couldn't take the pleasure anymore and started breathing heavy into her mouth. She pulled back from the kiss, and I saw her face mirrored mine. We were being driven past the point of no return, and we weren't even undressed.

The pleasure became too much for her, and she bit her lip as she fell into the crook of my neck, panting wildly. I was right behind her, losing my vision for a moment as my back arched and my hips curled against her.

It took a while before either of us could breathe normally again. When we could, she started laughing softy in my ear, sending another wave of pleasure through my happy parts. I really needed to change my pants.

"Wow," was all she said.

"You think?"

"Well, we didn't break any rules."

"No, but we bent the hell out of them."

"You complaining?"

"Hell, no," I answered truthfully.

"Good boy. How's your head?"

I blinked in shock. It had stopped hurting. The pills must have kicked in. "Much better."

"Good."

"How are you feeling?"

She laughed at the stupidity of my question. "Purrfect,"she said, and kissed my neck, rolling over into the crook of my arm again.

I had just started to relax when the doorbell rang. "Great," I sighed and kissed Fern quickly. "I'll be right back."

"I'll be right here."

The doorbell rang again, I rolled my eyes and walked quickly through the house. Detective James was standing there about to push the button for the third time.

"Dane. Mind if I come in?"

"Detective? Sure," I said, and moved out of the way for him to enter.

He didn't hesitate and strolled into the house, looking around like police officers had a way of doing. "Some interesting things happened last night…"

"Want to have a seat?" I pointed at the dining room table.

"Sure." He pulled out a chair closest to the wall and sat, folding his hands on the table in front of him.

"Did you find the Mustang?"

"I did! With the help of your principal. It turns out that one of the very best friends of a…" He pulled out a little black leather notebook and moved the page back far enough to read it. Another classic cop move. "A Trevor Johnson owns one. The young man's name is Billy Bishop. Do you know Billy, Dane?"

"Not by name, but I just transferred here. I might know him if I saw him."

"Well, that's not important right now. You didn't see who was driving the vehicle, anyway, did you?'

"No, sir. Just saw the guy who threw the bottle."

"Did this guy happen to look like Trevor Johnson?"

"He did. But there's no way I can be sure."

"Is that why you didn't give me his name? The boy who had been bullying you at school the day before? The same boy whose face you kicked in because he was picking on your girlfriend? The same boy whose girlfriend caused a scene in the lunchroom at school? The same girl who texted said boyfriend after your little verbal altercation? Those were some pretty harsh words you all exchanged in front of hundreds of witnesses."

"I don't understand. Am I in trouble?"

"That depends. Where were you last night?"

"Um… Here. In a medically induced sleep."

The detective frowned. "Was your mother home?"

"All night."

"What about your girlfriend." He consulted his notebook again. "Lucy Fern? That name sounds awfully familiar. Where was she last night?"

"Um. Here? She stayed the night last night. She was sick and missed school. Her aunt is out of town, so we're taking care of her."

"Your girlfriend. Spent the night here?"

"Yes," Fern said as she walked out in her hoodie. She hadn't bothered putting pants on.

The detective looked up and blinked. "I thought your name sounded familiar. We meet again."

"Hello, detective." She pulled out the chair next to me and sat. I blinked in confusion.

The detective must have detected my confusion. "Your Fern and I have met several times in the past. Interesting girlfriend you have there. Keep lighters and sharp objects away from her, please."

I remembered Santa's Village. "I don't understand, Detective. What is this all about?"

He held up his hand. "Just for the record, you were *both* here *all* night long?"

"Yes," we said in unison.

"And your mother can vouch for this?"

"Yes," I answered. "She has a tendency to watch us like a hawk with Fern in the room next to mine."

"I can understand that. Okay, then. Sorry for bothering you."

"Can you at least tell us what all this is about? If I'm going to be accused of something, I'd at least like to know what."

"Fair enough. You see, when we took Billy Bishop in for questioning, it took a while, but he finally gave Trevor Jones up. Told us everything about your verbal altercation with his girlfriend. How they waited for you to get out of school, and then they rolled up on you real quiet like. Billy swears it was just to scare you. He was pissed at Trevor for hitting you in the face. Had to scare him with an accessory to attempted murder charge. He gave up his friend to avoid all that."

"I still don't have any idea what this has to do with us?" I pointed at Fern and me.

"No. I can see that now. You see, Trevor was murdered last night…"

"Wait. What?"

"Trevor Johnson was murdered."

"How?"

"This is where it gets weird. Someone let a mountain lion or a bear *into* his house."

To say I was shocked would have been the understatement of the year. The guy was a dick, but didn't deserve to get mauled to death. "Um. I'm no *Criminal Minds* expert, but are you sure it was a murder? I mean wouldn't the more plausible explanation be that a mountain lion or bear got *into* his house, and he was killed?"

"We thought that at first, too. Until we found out his parents were knocked out and tied up in the garage. They didn't even get a look at who did it. Then the sick bastard brought the animal upstairs and let it loose in his room."

"So, you immediately thought it was me? Because he threw a beer bottle at me? You want to check my room for mountain lions or bears?"

"People don't get murdered like that without a reason, son. If anybody had a reason, it was you. For what it's worth, I'm glad it wasn't. I heard what his girlfriend said to you. I'm also sorry to hear about your father."

Even with being accused of murder, I wasn't really angry with the detective. He had a point. And he was a decent guy. "Thanks."

He nodded. "Well, I better start looking for escaped circus animals." He stood up and reached across the table. I shook his hand and got up to walk him to the front door. He paused a moment and looked at Fern. "*You*, stay out of trouble."

"I will."

"Sure, you will," he said, and rolled his eyes. He turned back to me. "*You*, keep her out of trouble."

"I can't even get her to wear pants."

"You poor thing," he chuckled. "Jesus, son. What kind of ointment are you using?"

"Excuse me?"

"Your forehead looked like a roadmap to Louisiana last night. Can barely see it now. Except for the stitches."

I reached up and felt it. He was right. The angry swelling had gone down, and I could barely feel the wound. It didn't even hurt. The only thing I *could* feel were the bumps where the stitches ridged my skin. "Just whatever the hospital gave me."

"Huh. That doc is pretty good."

"Apparently."

"Tell your mom I said hi."

"You know my mom?"

"Met her last night. Let her know I came and asked you a few questions. Don't like keeping stuff like that from the

115

parents. Technically, you're a minor, and she should have been here when I questioned you, but you didn't know that," he said with a wink.

"Slick." I said with a little laugh. I didn't mind at all. Since I was completely innocent.

"Have your mom call me if she wants to yell at me. I deserve it. But at least that's over."

"I will. I'll leave the part out where you accused me of being an animal tamer, though."

He tipped his imaginary hat. "See ya, kid."

"Stay safe, Detective."

CHAPTER 14

"Are you sure you're not a vampire or something? Healing that fast is…kind of superhuman."

The nurse who had been there when I woke up was working in the emergency room again, second night in a row. I got lucky. Mom had insisted on driving me over to have the wound looked at. The nurse took one look and pulled me back into the ER, leaving Mom and Fern in the waiting room.

"Yeah. Pretty sure, or at least I don't feel any craving for blood."

"Well, okay then. We'll just chalk it up to the wonders of youthful skin."

"I bet you have the same problem." I had no idea where the thought came from, but it popped out of my mouth before I could stop it. I wasn't one to flirt. Ever. But, the brunette nurse in her early twenties was completely gorgeous.

"You're slick."

"As concrete. I'm sorry, I have no idea where that came from."

"I'll let you in on a little secret. *Never* apologize for complimenting someone," she said with a little smile, snipping one of the stitches and pulling it free. She used two of her fingers to pull the scar apart before running her finger over it. "It's completely healed." She was staring at it, mouth agape.

"It doesn't hurt, either."

"I can see why now. It looks like you've had it for months instead of a day."

"That's good, right?"

"I'd say. I'll be right back. I'm going to find the doctor. I want him to take a look at it."

"Sure."

She wandered off into the ER. A few minutes later she came back, doctor in tow. "See?"

"Holy shit." He stopped in his tracks and shot me an apologetic look before reaching out and touching the scar on my forehead. Instead of using two fingers, he used both hands and tugged at the seams. "He's healed."

"I know," the nurse said impatiently.

"Dane, was it?"

I nodded.

"Are you sure you didn't put anything on it last night?"

"Positive. I barely made it into bed."

"Well, I'm at a loss. Mind if we take some tissue samples?"

"Will it hurt?"

"A little."

"Okay then," I said, rolling my eyes.

He turned back to the nurse. "Scrape some of the area around that and give it to me when you're done, if you will. I need to go set a leg."

He strolled out of my little cordoned-off area without so much as a "Bye."

"Be gentle," I told the nurse.

"I bet you say that to all the girls."

"That was my first time *ever* saying it. So, no."

She laughed and dug around the drawers before coming back with a little plastic vial with a lid in a pull-apart plastic wrap, and a scalpel, wrapped the same way. She donned a new pair of gloves and ripped open the packages.

I felt myself blushing as she worked, her face inches from mine. Everywhere I looked, all I could see was her. The front of her scrubs had bellowed out as she leaned over me. In an effort to be a gentleman, I focused on her lips. Her very soft-looking lips.

"You're staring."

"Can't really look anywhere else."

"And here I was thinking you found me attractive."

"I do. Very much so. Just trying hard not to look down your shirt."

She laughed. "And that is precisely *why* I wear tank tops underneath."

I glanced down and sighed in relief. "Thank you."

"You're a pretty sweet kid," she said, and glanced down before pulling another stitch out of my forehead. "Is that your girlfriend in the lobby?"

"Yes."

"She's adorable. I love her hair."

"Me, too. And thanks. I made her myself in the basement."

"Um. Okay."

"Hardest part was finding the one-point-twenty-one jiggawatts."

"You do know it's gigawatts, right?"

"Shhh. This is my fantasy."

"You fantasize about making women in your basement?"

"What seventeen-year-old doesn't? Sheesh."

"There. That's the last one. Now for the fun part."

I winced in pain before she even picked up the scalpel. "Easy, tiger. We're not even there yet."

"Don't like knives digging into my face. Call me weird."

She looked me in the eyes and whispered, "I'll be gentle and quick."

"That's what she said."

"You're right. I did."

She held the vial to my head and I heard, rather than felt, the blade scraping skin and some flecks of dried blood from one of the suture marks. She sealed the lid on the container and put everything down on the tray next to me.

"That's it?"

"That's it."

"But I hardly felt anything."

"That's what she said," she said, winking.

∞ ∞ ∞

"Three, please," Mom told the hostess.

"Follow me, please."

Mom immediately stepped forward, Fern and I following behind her. I glanced around the inside of the Crab Pot. Mom was celebrating my spectacular healing and Fern's quick recovery by treating us to seafood. She hadn't got the insurance money yet, but she was a little less worried about every dime she spent. I wasn't complaining.

"I've never had crabs," Fern said beside me.

"Good," I answered with a chuckle. She didn't get it, and I didn't explain. "You'll enjoy it more this way," I added, feeling bad about making a joke she didn't get.

"Are they good?"

"Very. I'm surprised you never put some in your bento boxes."

"I've had fake crab sticks. I use them a lot."

"That's like comparing sponges to sponge cake."

She shrugged as the hostess got us settled into a quiet table in the back. I hoped the food was good, the place wasn't exactly brimming with customers.

The ancient waitress, who sounded like she gargled with gravel every morning, took our drink order and shuffled off to get them. I laughed as I looked over the menu. "You sure about this, Mom? Cheapest thing on here is twenty dollars, and that's for chicken."

"I'm sure. It's been a while since we had a nice meal."

"Thank you for inviting me," Fern added, politely.

Mom beamed. "You're part of the family now, too. Don't forget it."

Fern wiped the corner of her eye, and I could tell it would be forever before she got used to it. I rubbed her leg under the table. She reached down and squeezed my hand.

"What do you think? Should we do the crab pot for three?"

"I'm game." I closed my menu and set it down next to me.

"What is a crab pot?" Fern's voice cracked, and it came out almost like a whisper.

"They boil crabs, potatoes, corn, and other stuff, and then bring the whole thing to the table. We share," I answered.

She nodded and closed her menu. I took it from her and set it on mine, sliding the stack to Mom to give to the waitress. I got the weird feeling someone was staring at us. Glancing around, I noticed Detective James sitting at the bar. I waved to him, and he smiled.

"Maybe I'm still a suspect," I whispered.

"What, honey?"

"The detective who questioned me is sitting at the bar."

Mom turned around and saw him sitting there. "I'll be right back." She stood and marched over to him.

I couldn't make out their conversation, but I could tell Mom must have accused him of tailing us from his pleading innocence look. He even had his hands up in the air. Mom put her hand on her hip and shifted her stance. He was in for it after that. I'd seen that look many times. I sat back and waited for the fireworks that never came.

She visibly relaxed, and then they both chuckled. I shifted in my seat uneasily, and I couldn't tell why.

My answer came a moment later when he stood up and followed Mom back to our table. "Dane, Fern," he said in greeting as he sat down next to Mom.

"Okay, he wasn't tailing you. He was actually sitting there when we walked in," Mom explained. "He looked sad and lonely, so I asked him to join us."

I remembered him being *too* interested in my mother from our conversation earlier. If I added that to the fact that he seemed *way* too happy sitting next to her, I could only come to the conclusion that life was about to become much more interesting. At least for Mom.

At first my hackles rose, but the detective seemed like a decent guy. As long as he wasn't married with kids, an alcoholic, or just a dick, I was happy for her. I couldn't help it though; I looked at his left hand. No sign of a ring or even a mark on his finger. "Hey, Detective."

"Brian. I'm not working right now."

"But Detective sounds so much cooler," I added.

He laughed and raised his glass. "Thanks. Unless you were making fun of my name, in which case I should let you know I do have handcuffs."

"My name is Dane. Do you think I would make fun of Brian?"

"Good point."

We both laughed.

"So, there's no Mrs. Detective?"

"Not for four years. She moved to Florida after the divorce."

"Ew. I don't think I could handle that heat," Mom added to the conversation. "We're going for the crab pot. Care to share?"

"Sounds good."

"You eat here a lot?" I was curious why he was at a bar in a seafood place. The restaurant was kind of fancy. And by fancy, I mean expensive.

"Quite often, actually. Not everybody in the family became a cop. My sister always liked cooking, so…"

"This is your sister's restaurant?"

He nodded at my mother. "Yep."

"I hope she gives you a discount."

"She charges me double. I was kind of a jerk to her when we were kids…"

Mom laughed. "I'll buy dinner then."

"You will not," he said firmly.

Mom blushed. She was kind of cute when she was flirty. I squeezed Fern's leg. She yelped. I had gotten her right above the knee. She blushed as everybody turned to look at her.

"Dane, behave yourself."

"I am! I just squeezed her knee," I said and did it again to show her. Fern yelped and jumped again. "See?"

Fern swatted me in the arm, reached down and slid my hand farther up her thigh. I didn't mind at all.

The waitress came back with the drinks for the three of us, finally. I had a feeling it was going to be a long dinner.

"You sitting over here, Chief?"

"Hey, Tammy. Yes. We're going to do the crab pot for four. Tell Sissy to go heavy with the Old Bay and bring us a bottle of white wine, two glasses."

She wrote it down and shuffled off again. I assumed it would be an hour or two by the time she got the order into the kitchen. "She seems nice and efficient."

"Tammy?"

I nodded.

"She was my sister's first grade teacher. Gave her a job when she retired."

"That's ridiculously sweet," I said, blinking.

"I know, right? Very unusual for my sister…"

The tall blonde, who had walked up to our table, slapped him in the back of the head. "Quit talking about me when I'm not here to defend myself, Bri."

"Sorry, Suzy." He sounded contrite, even if the smile on his face said otherwise.

"Hi. Welcome to the Crab Pot. I see you know my degenerate brother."

"Yes. We met at the hospital the other night," Mom said, and offered her hand.

"I hope under good circumstances." His sister seemed a little surprised.

"My son was attacked by a teenager with a beer bottle."

Not how I pictured the conversation starting. "Then he accused me of murder," I added, just for kicks.

She slapped him in the back of the head again. I liked his sister. Even Fern chuckled. He finally threw his arms over his head. "And you can forget the extra Old Bay. Not with your ulcer."

"What am I, twelve?"

"Sometimes I think you are. It was nice meeting you all. I've got your pot on the fire," she said, and moved on to the next table.

"She seems nice," Mom said with a snicker.

CHAPTER 15

Fern and I walked up to the school, holding hands and laughing. It felt a little more tolerable going back with her. I had no idea what the mood would be with Trevor's passing. I'm sure I wouldn't be the only one looking forward to not having to deal with him, but I'm sure the football team and Valerie might have a different view. I at least had the morals to feel bad that I was happy he was gone. But nobody, and I mean nobody, deserved to get eaten by a bear.

I grabbed the handle of the door and pulled it open for Fern. She slipped inside, and I let it close behind me. Principal Edwards had taken up his usual post by the door, even though we were almost early for once. I briefly wondered if he stood there all morning.

"Morning, sir," I said, and walked past him.

"How are you feeling?"

"Better, now that I got my stitches out."

He nodded, not commenting on my miraculous recovery. "I'm also sorry to hear about your father. You had a rough week."

"Just a little. Here's hoping for a better one."

"Stay out of trouble," he said, and went back to watching the entrance.

Fern tugged on my hand, dragging me away from the principal. I think she was a little uncomfortable in his presence. I didn't blame her; she hadn't had the most illustrious school career. The dean probably flinched whenever he saw her.

"He's pretty nice for a principal," I told her as we walked down the hall toward homeroom.

"Still the principal. They're evil."

I chuckled softly enough that she couldn't hear me. Most people probably thought the same thing about her. I didn't because I knew her, but most people probably wouldn't have warm and cozy feelings for someone who set fire to Santa's Village.

A few people in the halls openly stared at us as we made our way to class, but nobody spoke to us. The group of cheerleaders standing in a semicircle, sans Valerie, shot us contemptuous glances and whispered. One of them even frantically tapped on the keys of her phone screen.

"Hurry," Fern said worriedly, as if she could sense the calm before the storm.

"Relax. Everything will be okay," I whispered like I actually believed the words coming out of my mouth.

We made it into homeroom without incident. It almost felt surreal. It had been that long since Fern and I had been to school together. I got her settled at her desk and sat in mine, flipping through my phone.

I'm bored. It had taken all of two minutes for Fern to text me from across the room.

Homeroom is quick. We'll be in English Lit soon. At least we'll be next to each other.

They're staring.

I looked up and, sure enough, the entire class was either staring at Fern or looking at me.

"What?" I asked the entire class.

They all turned around and found things that could qualify as interesting on their desks. I sighed in frustration. Finally, Mr. Johnson came in and things relaxed. By the time the first bell rang, I was almost back to my usual, chipper self. That ended when the first football player shoulder-checked me in the hallway on the way to class.

Fern tried to spin around, but I held her hand. She looked down at it and back up at me for an explanation. "Not worth it. Day will go by quickly. And the next one. And the one after that. Let it go."

She sighed. I could feel the tension in her hand, like she would claw the face of anyone else who dared lay a hand on me. She didn't do it to emasculate me or make me feel inadequate, she wanted to protect me. I hated to admit it, but it made me feel better.

I leaned over and kissed her ear in the hallway, "I love you," I whispered as I pulled away.

She blinked in surprise. I'd teased her the last time I told her. This time, I was forthright and meant every little word. All three of them.

"I love you, too." She sounded distant and surprised, quickly glancing around to see if anybody heard her.

I personally didn't care if they did. I'd shout it off the rooftop if she asked me to.

Fern gave me a smile and focused her attention ahead of us. It's probably what saved me from getting flattened by the bald jock swerving right in front of me. It was an attempt to humiliate me by knocking me back on my ass. Fern put an end to that by side-stepping and yanking on my hand. The jock lurched forward, completely missing me and falling flat on his face.

"Are you okay?" I asked, not really caring.

"Screw you, dickwad." He got up of the floor and pulled his arm back to throw a punch.

"Mr. Danvers. Come with me now." Dean Winchester's voice cut through the air in the hallway like a steel knife.

Danvers never got the time to swing. I watched his face crumple as he realized how screwed he was. His anger melted away, and he sighed heavily, shoulders drooping and fist falling to his side. He shot me a dirty look before he followed the dean down to his office. Ten minutes later, sitting in class, Fern and I listened as Dean Winchester came over the intercom, requesting that all members of the football team to please come down to his office.

Everyone in class looked at me. A few of them were smiling. I shrugged and continued reading the section we'd been assigned.

∞ ∞ ∞

"You ready to go home?"

Fern nodded and pressed her head against my shoulder as I unlocked my locker. Putting my unneeded books inside, I grabbed my Trig book and stuffed it into my bag. I slammed the locker shut and clicked the lock closed.

"Come on." I grabbed her hand and headed for the exit.

"I'm tired," Fern mumbled behind me.

Worried she was suffering a relapse, I stopped and kissed her forehead. "You're pretty warm, but not like the other day. Maybe you just overdid it. We'll get you some ibuprofen."

She shrugged and nodded, her eyes half-lidded.

"You going to make it?"

She nodded again.

"Want me to carry you?"

"No. But, let's hurry."

"Okay," I said, and opened the door.

The temperatures had risen a little, and I pulled my jacket off, draping it over my arm. Fern hugged my arm again, and we headed home. We had just made it off school property when she started shivering against me. I stopped us again and put my jacket over her hoodie. I doubted it would help, but it was better than nothing.

"Thanks," she mumbled half incoherently.

"Come on. Let's get you home and into bed."

She made a purring noise, and I couldn't help but laugh. Even sick, she was still cute. "Soup?"

"Yes. I'll make you some soup. And some tea."

She nodded against me.

We passed the park and headed down our street. We almost made it to the first house when Fern picked her head off my shoulder and sniffed the air. Her focus shifted ahead, and I saw Danvers step out from between two houses, heading in our direction.

"Let's cross the street," I said, and moved toward the road.

Danvers matched our movement. Apparently, he had no intention of letting us avoid him. I sighed. This was getting old, pretty quickly. Instead of continuing walking, we stopped and waited for him.

"Two days, asshole."

"How long it takes you to do math homework? The amount of time needed to find your junk to take a leak? Am I getting warm?"

His face contorted, and he closed the distance between us. "No. That's how long I got suspended for that little stunt you pulled in front of Winchester."

"The stunt I pulled? You tried to clothesline me and then took a swing at me! You're going to blame me?" I gently pushed Fern behind me. She was in no shape to fight. I could take the pounding if it would keep her safe.

"Screw you. Everybody knows you let a wild animal into Trevor's house. You're lucky I don't kill you."

"Again. I was laid up in bed because of the beer bottle he threw at my face."

"Where was your little girlfriend?"

"At home with me, sick in bed."

He stopped, confusion clearly etched upon his face. "Wait. You *live* together."

Shit.

"She's staying with us while her aunt is out of town. Problem?"

He had gotten close enough to throw a punch. I stared up at him. He had me by more than a half-a-foot and a hundred pounds. This was going to be over quickly. His nostrils flared, but he wasn't beating the crap out of me. I took it as a good sign.

"Then why is Valerie telling everybody she saw you walking down his street when she left?"

"Probably to piss you guys off. Who knows? She tried to get me in trouble with Winchester by passing a note that looked like I wrote it. She got her boyfriend to throw a beer bottle at my head. She's got every football player in the school shoulder blocking me in every hallway. She walks by me and makes snide comments about my dad dying. I don't know what the hell her problem is, but she just needs to let shit go. I don't want anything to do with her."

Danvers' twelve brain cells struggled to process the information I'd given him. I could almost smell smoke when the light went on in the attic. His eyebrows scrunched together, and he looked *pissed*, but not at me.

"You know Winchester pulled the entire football team into his office. We were told that the next person who even *looks* at you was going to be banned from playing football this year."

"What?"

He nodded. "That's the reason you don't have a dent in your face right now. I was just going to yell at you. I'm glad I didn't say screw it and do it anyway."

"Me, too."

He frowned again. "I can't believe she'd do that."

I assumed he was talking about Valerie. I couldn't believe he couldn't believe it. It didn't take a rocket scientist to figure out what a bitch she was. "She's… Valerie isn't a very nice person."

"No shit. It doesn't take a rocket scientist to figure that out," he said conspiratorially, echoing my thoughts. It was kind of creepy. "She was playing the sympathy card with us about Trev." He reached out and put his hand on my shoulder. "I'm sorry for earlier."

My mouth fell open in shock. "Hey. That's okay, don't worry about it."

"I'll tell the guys on the team what you told me. Most of them are too afraid to get kicked off anyway, but this will guarantee it. We do not like being played."

I nodded. "Sorry you got suspended."

"No worries." He took his hand off my shoulder and nodded, shoving his hands in his letterman jacket and heading back toward the way we came.

I shook my head, mentally unprepared to deal with the amount of drama I'd been subjected to. It was like a scene from a teen drama show. Just without any vampires.

"You okay, baby?" I turned to check on Fern, whose head hadn't left my back the entire time.

Her mouth was open and she panted, her face contorted with pain. She shook her head and looked up at me. Even in the afternoon sunlight, her eyes had a peculiar glow to them. I gulped and lowered my head down to hers. The glow vanished. I looked at the sun behind us. "Your eyes are pretty glassy. The sun made them look like they were on fire. Let's go."

She nodded and hung on to me as we walked briskly back home. I would have run if I thought she wouldn't have collapsed halfway. We finally made it, and I nearly kicked the front door open in my frustration of unlocking it.

Fern stumbled as we got inside. I caught her before she hit the ground and hoisted her up. She wrapped her arms around my neck, holding on for dear life. Awkwardly, I stumbled through the house and got her into my bed, falling with her. It put us in a precarious position, but she was sick enough, I was more worried than turned on.

"Let go, sweetie," I whispered. "You're home. I'll go make you some tea and soup."

Fern's legs loosened their grip and I tried to stand, but her arms were still wrapped around my neck. She wasn't letting go. "No. Stay."

"You don't want soup?"

"No. You."

I chuckled and said, "Okay."

She let go and rolled onto her side. I hadn't made the bed, so she wasn't on top of the comforter. I pulled it up over her and turned around.

"What are you doing?"

"Changing. I wanted to be comfortable," I said over my shoulder, undoing my belt and kicked my jeans off.

I grabbed the pair of light gray sweats I had slept in the night before, pulling them on and crawling under the covers with her. We had an hour or two before my mother got home from work.

I put one arm under her head and the other over her stomach, tugging her close and resting my head behind hers. She lifted her arm and settled her hand over mine, tucking it into her chest. I tried to ignore how warm and soft her flesh was under my palm. Luckily, she still had her hoodie on. She must have sensed my contentment, letting go and unzipping it before moving my hand back where it was. I held my hand very still, not even daring to flex my fingers as the heat of her flesh warmed my palm. I rolled my eyes and thought of math. It was the only thing I could do.

Finally, we both drifted off to sleep.

CHAPTER 16

I woke up hot. I think I may have actually snorted myself awake. A stray lock of purple hair wafted up my nose, and I sneezed. Fern didn't wake up. I lay my head back down on the pillow and smiled, burning into my memory that exact moment, how she felt in my arms, how she smelled, and how happy I felt being the one holding her.

My hand had drifted off her chest sometime while we were sleeping and was on her stomach. Her T-shirt had ridden up over and my hand was just below her bellybutton. Her skin burned under my touch, and I couldn't help myself, I began lightly tracing circles over her flesh.

She backed up, her butt nestled in firmly against me. Her hips began to match the rhythm of my hand. The inside of my sweatpants gliding over every part of me. My breathing picked up pace, as did hers.

"Please tell me you're awake," I said softly.

I felt her nod against my arm.

"Do you want me to stop?"

"Never," she almost moaned. She brought her shoulder back and tilted her head toward me. My lips found hers, and we kissed. This time, my tongue darted into her mouth, entwining with hers as we panted into each other's mouth. The feeling of closeness was overwhelming. She reached down and pushed my hand lower. She had kicked off her leggings at some point, and I felt the top of her panties.

"Fern."

"Don't you dare."

I nodded and let my hand glide over her and over her legs and back up, making lazy patterns all over her flesh. Her ass pressed up against me and began to buck furiously. The heat under the blanket exploded as I cried out, grinding myself against her. The front door opened and closed, and my mother called my name.

"No friggin' way."

Fern just chuckled lazily next to me.

I quickly lifted the comforter over me and tucked it in between us. "Pretend to be asleep."

She nodded ever so slightly.

Mom came into my room as I rolled over and made shushing motions with my finger. She looked at Fern, concernedly.

"She got sick on the way home from school. She almost passed out," I whispered over my shoulder.

"Poor thing. Stay with her, I'll bring in the groceries. If she keeps getting sick, I'm going to take her to the doctor."

I smiled. "Thanks, Mom."

"I got some frozen pizzas for dinner, that okay?"

"Yeah. That actually sounds good."

"Okay, baby. Take care of her."

"Always."

Mom flashed a quick smile and closed the door, and I began hyperventilating.

"You okay?" Fern's whisper made me laugh.

"No. I need to change my pants for a couple of reasons." I slid out of bed and walked over to my dresser, pulling out a clean pair of pants and boxers. I made a rolling motion to Fern, and she smiled before turning over and facing the wall.

I threw the dirty ones in the laundry and crawled back into bed, laying my arm over her and holding her again. "That was amazing. Again."

"Imagine how it would feel if we actually did it."

"I can't. I'd probably die."

"Maybe," she whispered.

"Be worth it, though." I kissed her cheek. "How you feeling?"

"Better now."

"That's the second time…"

"Yes, it was. Both were good."

"I meant that you felt better…after…"

"Yeah. Just needed to recharge the old battery, I guess."

"Well, act sick around Mom."

"Okay."

We lay there until the smell of pizza became impossible to ignore. My stomach was growling, causing Fern to giggle. "Sue me, I'm hungry."

"Go eat."

"You're not hungry?"

She shook her head.

"I thought you were feeling better?"

"I'm not in pain. I feel much, much better. I'm just not hungry."

"Okay. Want some soup?"

"You don't mind?"

"Taking care of you? Never…"

She smiled and turned to peck me on the lips. "Just a cup."

"Will do."

∞ ∞ ∞

Sleep eluded me. Something was nagging at my conscious and I didn't know what it was. It felt like I'd forgotten something or wasn't getting the whole picture. I couldn't imagine what it could be or what it even concerned.

Sighing for the hundredth time, I flipped over on the air mattress.

I was back in Fern's room. She had fallen asleep again in my bed, and I didn't have the heart to wake her up. Mom shot me a look when I mentioned I should sleep in there to keep an eye on her. I'd meant it, too. I was starting to worry about her.

The sounds of the bathroom door opening and closing, and then the shower starting, broke me out of my reverie. She must have woken up and wanted to get clean. She'd been sweating pretty badly earlier.

I closed my eyes and listened to the sound of the water splashing on the shower floor. It reminded me of rain and almost lulled me back to sleep. The sounds of a couple of moans woke me right back up. I blushed, thinking about what she could be doing in the shower.

Eventually the water stopped and then silence, until the sliding sound of the shower door opening echoed through the wall. I had to pee; I hoped she hurried up.

Rolling off the bed and onto the floor, I lifted myself up quietly. I wanted a quick kiss before going back to bed. I opened the bedroom door and waited for her to come out. Finally, the bathroom door opened, and Fern stepped out, turning to my bedroom without so much as a backward glance at me. She didn't notice me standing there.

That's the precise moment when I noticed she wasn't wearing anything but a towel. Oh, and there were leathery black wings sprouting from her back.

I wanted to call out to her. I wanted to scream. I wanted to turn around and go back to bed and pretend the whole thing had been a dream. I also found myself wanting to run. Instead, I waited until she slipped into my bedroom and gently shut the door behind her.

My girlfriend wasn't human.

Then reality came crashing down. Trevor's death. The demonic paintings on the ceiling of her house. Her mother's insanity. So many other little things that I'd missed, just started making sense and filling in the puzzle.

I didn't know what to do or where to even start. Not having a clue, I waited a few minutes and then walked into the bathroom, peed, and went back to the bed in Fern's room where I spent the remainder of the night staring at the ceiling.

One realization came to me in five hours of internal contemplation. I was too stupid to be afraid. I'd spent my life standing up to everybody. It had gotten my ass kicked more often than not, but at least I had. It would be no different with Fern. Her secret had gotten out; I'd seen her without her hoodie and T-shirt. What I thought was a horribly misshapen back was actually carefully folded wings. She might lash out at me for seeing her, but I would deal with it.

Eventually Mom popped her head into the room. "I'm heading to work. Have fun at school."

"I think I caught what Fern has. I feel like shit. Staying home today."

She hurried into the room and kissed my forehead. "Well at least you don't have a fever. Do you need me to pick up anything from the store or need anything before I go?"

"No. I should be fine. I'll text you if I need you."

"Okay, honey. I'm assuming Fern will stay home then."

"Yeah. Probably. Geniuses don't need to go to school every day."

"I wish some of that would rub off on you."

"Yeah. Me, too."

"Alright, honey. Feel better."

"Love you, Mom."

"Now, I know you're sick," she said with a laugh, and headed out the door.

No. I just don't know if I'll ever see you again, I replied in my head.

As soon as the front door slammed shut and Mom's car revved from the driveway, I was left alone in the house with the demon in my bed. I flung the covers off and went to my room, sitting in my desk chair after turning it toward the bed.

I watched her for a few minutes. She was awake. I don't know how I knew, but I did. I didn't know where to start. I didn't know how to tell her I knew what she was. Eventually, I didn't have to. She might have taken pity on me or wanted to get everything out in the open. Either way, she rolled over, tears staining her cheeks.

I wanted to go to her, wipe away her tears and kiss her. Tell her everything would be all right. I wished I didn't have to pee last night, I really did.

"You saw."

I nodded.

Her tears turned into wracking sobs that she couldn't contain. She rolled over on her stomach and wailed into my pillow. I wanted to comfort her, but I didn't know if I could go to her. Not without knowing if she killed Trevor.

"Did you do it?"

She stopped sobbing and looked up at me. Demon tears and demon snot ran down her face and onto my pillow. "Do what?"

"Did you kill Trevor?"

"Is that what you think of me?"

"No. But you didn't think enough of me to tell me the truth. I'm asking you because I want to hear it from you. Did you kill Trevor?"

"No!"

I thanked everybody from God to the demons in hell.

"Thank you."

"You believe me? Just like that?" She blinked at me in disbelief.

"Would you lie to me?"

"Not about that."

"What would you lie to me about?"

"Um… Wings, obviously."

"Anything else? Do you really love me?"

"Do you always ask this many questions?"

"Only when I find out the girl I love isn't exactly human."

"In my defense, I am half."

I sighed. Things started making even more sense. "Your mom is human."

"Yes. It's why I have trouble controlling my powers. And why I can't make my wings go away."

"Full demons can?"

"Yes. They're pretty amazing. Scary and intense, but amazing."

I almost put my feet up on the bed, this was going to be a long talk or a quick death. "You want some coffee?"

Fern looked at me like *I* was the crazy one. Maybe I was.

"Do you want me to leave?"

"Would you?"

She nodded, and the tears started rolling down her face again.

"No. I don't want you to leave."

"Why?"

"Because I'm scared."

"Of me?"

"Of losing you."

"You don't think I'm a hideous monster?"

That kind of broke my heart. I got up and moved over to the bed. She backed away. The girl who could kick a football player's ass was afraid of me. I turned around and lay back on the bed, my head right next to her stomach.

"Can I be honest?"

"Yes."

"I was shocked. The truth is I expected your back to be a mass of wounds inflicted by your mother. I was expecting misshapen bones, scars, you name it."

"I wish that was it. It would have been easier to tell you than the truth."

"Is that what you think?"

"Obviously."

I rolled over on my elbow and reached out gently to put my hand on her leg. She didn't flinch away this time. "Let me ask you one more thing before we continue. Did you *want* to tell me?"

"Only a thousand times. The first time I took my hoodie off for you, I almost did. I *really* wanted to. I just… If you… I couldn't. I wanted to, but I couldn't."

I put myself in her place for a moment. If I weren't human, my mother had gone insane, and my aunt had left. If I were alone in the world, never seemed to get along with anyone, kept getting in trouble with the law, and then I found somebody who saw the real me. If I wasn't alone anymore, and I'd found someone who told me they loved me… Would I have been able to tell them, to show them? I'd be a fricking liar if I said yes.

"Fern. I'm sorry. I'm sorry I asked if you had anything to do with Trevor's death. I *really* didn't think you did it. I was just afraid."

"Of me." She didn't make it a question.

"No. Of not being able to love you."

"What?"

"I was afraid of having to let you go. Murder… Yeah. I don't know if I could handle that. I was afraid of being unable to love you. Of losing you."

"Do you mean that?"

"Yes," I said instantly.

"Do you think I'm hideous?"

I laughed at her. She blinked in confusion. I scooted closer to her and lay my head in her lap, turning to face her. "I answered *that* question a while ago. I told you there wasn't a spot on your body I *wouldn't* find insanely attractive. That includes your wings. You know, the ones I didn't know were there," I said, and poked her in the tummy.

"Show me."

"My wings? I don't have any."

She rolled her eyes in frustration. "Show me you don't think they're hideous. Show me you don't think I'm a misshapen freak. Show me you don't hate me."

"That's easy."

"How?"

I got up and reached my hand out to her. She stared at it for a moment before she took it. I pulled her from my room and into the bathroom, flipping on the light as I entered. When we were inside, I turned her to face the mirror and stood behind her, looking over her shoulder so she could see my face. She opened her mouth to speak, but I shook my head, silencing her.

"Now keep your eyes on my face."

She nodded, and I looked away from the mirror, focusing on her shoulder, leaning in and kissing her neck. I reached around her, grabbing the hoodie from the front and peeled it back. I tugged it down off her shoulders and off her arms. She crossed them over her chest, standing there in her T-shirt and panties.

I stepped closer to her, feeling the bones in her wings touching my chest. I'd felt them before, but now I knew what they were. How I hadn't figured it out before, boggled my mind. Knowing what they were, I could see them clearly even through her shirt.

Love is blind.

I wrapped my arms around her stomach, leaning in and kissing her cheek, her temple, her neck. I could feel her relaxing against me. I opened my hands and put my palms against her stomach, sliding them down and curling them over the hem of her shirt. She began to shake her head and panic.

"It's okay. I *want* to see you."

She uncrossed her arms slowly as I lifted her shirt up and over her stomach. When I reached the bottom of her breasts, she lifted her arms over her head. I didn't stop, and I didn't stop looking at her in the mirror as I lifted the shirt up and off, tossing it to the ground at our feet. I kissed her neck one more time before standing back and staring at the both of us in the mirror.

I imagined seeing her breasts for the first time would have gone a lot different than this, but I wasn't going to complain. She was absolutely gorgeous. I stepped back again until my back was against the wall. I tore my eyes away from hers and *looked* at her back.

Her skin was flawless, not a single blemish marred the surface. Tiny white hairs ran down her neck and sprinkled lightly across her shoulders. They made me smile as I imagined running my lips over them. I let my gaze travel lower and saw where the wings sprouted from her shoulder blades. The flesh of her back darkened until it became midnight black. The wings themselves were smaller than I'd imagined and were *nothing* like a bat's. The main bone was thick, but not that long, and ended in a barbed claw. The bone was arched as well, not straight like I would have expected. From there three jointed bones spread toward the floor, a thick, leathery membrane stretched between them. The knuckles of the wing joints must have allowed her to fold them up, keeping them out of sight and tucked up under her hoodie.

The skin was black and almost sparkled under the overhead vanity light. If you stared long enough, they resembled a field of stars. I leaned over and gently kissed the joint on her back, glancing up into the mirror for permission. She nodded, tears becoming an endless stream as they poured, not rolled, down her face.

I slid the tips of my fingers up the right wing, mesmerized by the softness and beauty of it. She shuddered under my touch and opened her mouth a little.

"Does that tickle?"

She shook her head. "No. It feels...amazing. You're the first person who has ever touched me there."

"This wasn't the scenario I pictured when I imagined you finally saying that to me." I gave her a wink. "Holy shit!"

For the first time *ever,* I had made Fern blush. I would relish that feeling for a long, long time. I smiled and kissed her wing as I ran my fingers down the other bones. She groaned and leaned back against me.

"You are beautiful," I whispered into her ear as she rolled her head against my shoulder. I slid my hands all over her, and not just her wings. For the first time, I cupped her breasts and ran my fingers over them as well. "I wish you had shown me sooner. I'm sorry you were afraid. Nobody should be ashamed of who they are, especially you."

She folded her wings in a swift motion and spun, grabbing my face and kissing me in the bathroom in her underwear. Then, she shut off the light.

CHAPTER 17

We were lying on my bed when my phone rang. Grabbing it off my nightstand, I saw the detective's name flash across the screen. "Detective James?"

"Dane?"

"Yeah. What can I do for you?"

"Are you home or at school?"

"Fern and I are home. Everything okay?"

"No. Mind if I come over?"

"Do I need to have my mom here?"

"No. I called her already."

That sounded ominous. "Sure, come on over. Want coffee?"

"If you have some."

"Well, you *did* buy us dinner. I could put some on. I'm sure Fern will have some, too."

"Sounds good."

I hung up the phone and looked at the very naked Fern, snuggled under my covers. "You may want to put some clothes on, the detective is coming over."

"Someone else is dead."

I blinked in confusion. "How do you know?"

"I can feel it. I knew when Trevor was murdered, too."

"Why didn't you say anything?"

"Would you have believed me? Would you have believed me and *not* suspected me?"

"Fern. I don't know if you know this, but some pretty outrageous stuff flies out of your mouth on a regular basis. No, I wouldn't have been shocked. I probably would have believed you, and no, I wouldn't have suspected you at all."

"Sure," she said with a light chuckle. She slid out from under the covers, and I didn't avert my gaze. I don't think I ever could again. I'd become too fascinated by her flesh. All of it.

"Wow."

"What?"

"You're hot."

She looked down at the blanket covering me and laughed. "So are you. Put some pants on and make me some coffee."

"Yes, ma'am," I said and got up, stopping by the bathroom to grab my pants on the way. I hopped to the kitchen, putting them on. I had just grabbed a coffee pod when the doorbell rang.

I walked over and opened it. It was raining, and the detective looked miserable. "Were you parked in front of the house when you called?"

"Yeah. Kinda."

I laughed and let him in. "Was just making coffee."

"Black, please."

"You and Fern. Sickos."

"Don't like it black?"

"Don't like it." I shoved the pod in the maker and opened the fridge, pulling out my morning Coke.

"Now, *that's* just gross."

I shrugged, popped the top, and took a swig, setting it down on the counter next to the coffee maker. I burped and handed the detective his mug before putting another on for my girlfriend.

"So, what's up?"

He held up his hands. "I just want to confirm with you *both*," he looked at Fern as she walked into the room, "and I'm sorry I have to ask. But you were *both* here all night, correct?"

"Yes," we said in unison. I guess Fern was right. There had been another murder.

"Why?" I tried to keep the suspicion out of my voice.

"There was another murder last night. Another one of your classmates that you had an altercation with at school."

"Danvers," I said, guessing.

"Yes. While questioning some of the students and teachers, your fight was mentioned several times."

"Of course it was. He nearly beat me to a pulp."

"That was the general consensus, yes," he said with a chuckle.

"I bet nobody told you that I ran into him after school, and we talked it out. He even told me he was going to let the rest of the football team know not to harass me anymore."

"No. They didn't. Your mother did, though. I'm glad you told her about it. That was well before the TOD."

"TOD?"

"Time of death. No. I don't think you did it. Just had to ask."

"Wait, you already talked to Mom?"

"Yes. I called her first. I didn't want to upset her by questioning you again without her knowledge. She let me off the hook the first time…"

The detective was a smart man.

"So, she already told you we were both here all night."

He sipped his coffee. "Yeah. I just wanted to hear it from you. Makes my job easier."

I thought about that for a moment. "So, if anything comes of it, you don't have one statement, you have multiple statements corroborating."

"Yep," he answered, impressed. "You'd make a good cop."

"No. My dad was a lawyer."

He nodded, solemnly. I guessed Mom had told him the story. They talked a lot more than I imagined. I was kind of happy about it.

I turned to Fern. She had stopped mid-sip and was staring at the counter. "You okay?"

Her head bobbed and set the mug down. "That's twice. Twice you got into a fight. Twice that person ended up dead. That can't be a coincidence. How was Danvers killed, if you don't mind my asking?"

Fern was a genius. I knew it for a fact. I'd seen her chew schoolwork up and spit it out in her head. However, hearing her speak, half the time you would *never* guess a genius resided in that cute head of hers. When she spoke this time, she sounded calm, analytical, and *highly* intelligent. I wondered, and not for the first time, how much of her insanity act was an act. Maybe it was easier to keep people away feigning crazy.

"Same MO. Mauled to death by some sort of animal."

"Anybody home besides him this time?"

"Mother. Knocked unconscious and tied up. No chance this was someone else."

"Let's just hope Valerie doesn't start spreading rumors that she saw me by Danvers' house. I don't feel like getting mauled by the football team again."

"What?"

I looked up at the detective. "Trevor's girlfriend, the cheerleader captain, told the entire football team she had seen me walking toward Trevor's house the night he was murdered."

"Why am I just hearing about this now?"

"Because I didn't know until I talked to Danvers. He asked me what I was doing there if I didn't kill him. I told him Valerie was lying, and that I had witnesses to me being home all night."

He nodded and took another sip of coffee. "Think this Valerie might have something to do with it?"

"I doubt it. It was her boyfriend who was killed, and the rest of the football team does her bidding. Or did. I'll let you know how school goes tomorrow…"

"Please do."

"At least the dean seems to be on my side. He threatened to keep anybody who harassed me off the football team this year."

"Good. All right, well, I should be going. Thanks for the coffee."

"My pleasure."

He stood up, looked like he wanted to say something else, but instead just nodded, heading for the front door "Bye, Fern. See ya, Dane."

"Have a good one."

I walked him to the front door and shut it behind him, locking it for good measure. By the time I got back into the kitchen, Fern was making herself another cup of coffee and staring absentmindedly off into space. "You okay?"

She shook her head.

"Still feeling sick?"

"No. There's another demon."

I thought she was joking for a moment, but it made sense. Too much sense. Highly unusual for Fern. "Wait. You're serious?"

"Yes," she answered, pulling her mug from the maker and taking a slow sip. "I felt it last night, briefly, when it killed Danvers. I *thought* I felt it when Trevor died, too. There is no wild animal killing people."

"Shit."

She nodded.

"And you've never had that feeling when you're at school?"

"No. Only when they kill. It's why I felt disgusted last night and had to take a shower. I couldn't get rid of the feeling."

"Maybe that's why you were feeling sick?"

She shrugged.

"So, you can't just walk around with your demon radar and figure out who is doing this."

"No. I wish I could, but it doesn't work that way. Especially if they're in their human seeming."

"Human seeming?" I had a feeling I was about to get a lesson in demonology. I grabbed my Coke and sat in front of Fern at the counter.

She nodded. "Yes. Demons can make their wings disappear, or at least make it *look* like they do. They can also hide their talons and horns."

I took a big gulp of Coke. "And you can't because you're half human…"

She paused, but nodded. "Mostly."

"Mostly?"

"Promise not to freak?"

My eyes narrowed. "Yes."

She held up her hands and concentrated on them. It took a moment, but her fingernails started to grow longer and became a full set of claws. She *clicked* them loudly against the Formica counter. The skin around her claws darkened, too. Almost matching the flesh of her wings.

"They're kind of gross."

"Would you do me a favor?"

It was her turn to narrow her eyes suspiciously. "What?"

"I have this itch… Would you mind?" I pointed at my back. Her mouth dropped open as she stared at me incredulously. "I'm kidding! They're not gross at all."

She sighed and rolled her eyes. "Say that about these."

150

Once again, I could see her lost in concentration as she pulled the hair back from her face, exposing her forehead. Wincing in pain, her eyes closed as two horns slowly grew, pushing through the skin of her forehead. They stopped after a couple of inches, not at all as large as I was expecting. But they were black and ridged, and kind of cute. I smiled at her. "Still not gross. Kind of cute, actually."

She almost blushed. "Pervert."

I laughed and didn't deny it. "How come you can make those disappear, but not your wings?"

"I don't know. I was born with horns and tail. The talons came later. The wings when I was ten. Since I'm half, I imagine I *will* be able to one day, just not yet."

"Holy shit. Did you just say you have a *tail*?"

She nodded, clearly afraid.

"Can I?"

"No."

"Why?"

"You'll hate it. It's gross."

"Yeah. Like the wings, talons, and horns that I find attractive?"

"You do not. You're just being…you."

"Fern," I said sternly. "I won't lie to you. I *do* find them attractive. Especially the horns."

She blinked at me.

I went back to the kitchen and stood in front of her. I lifted my hand to her face and ran my finger along one horn. The tip wasn't sharp, much to my surprise. I leaned in and kissed her lips.

Her talons, on the other hand, *were* sharp. She needed to be careful with those… "Ouch," I said in surprise.

"Yes. Sharp."

"Just a tad, but still not gross." I curled her fingers around my hand and brought them to my lips, leaving a kiss where each talon met her finger.

"You're not just saying that?"

"I don't know how many times I'll have to say it before you believe it. *I think you are beautiful. All* of you."

Something tapped my shoulder. I looked over, and a black arrow-tipped tail waved at me. Glancing down, I noticed she had lowered her leggings over her butt behind her.

"Holy shit."

"See!"

"That's friggin' *hot*."

"You're insane," she whispered. "It's like… It's…"

"Can I touch it?"

"No!"

"Why?"

"It's really… It's sensitive." She lowered her eyes in embarrassment. I gripped it lightly, laughing as it wiggled in my hand. I stroked my finger along the tip, and she nearly fell to the ground as she quivered.

"Oh! *That* kind of sensitive. I'm sorry. I thought you meant ticklish."

She gave me an exasperated stare, and the tail pulled out of my hands, curled up her back, and wrapped around her neck. "Don't do that ever again."

Shame colored my cheeks. "I'm so sorry." I held out my hands in apology.

"I should have been more specific. You didn't know. I'm sorry, too." She wrapped her arms around me.

"Not going to lie, though. That was fun. I kind of want to do it again."

"There's other spots you can touch. Not the tip of my tail."

"What about later…"

"Dane. It feels so good it hurts."

"Oh. What about if I just lightly kissed it?"

"Gently!"

152

I pulled back and watched as her tail unwrapped itself from around her neck. The tip peeked at me from over her shoulder. It seemed almost alive, sentient, and afraid. Slowly, it worked its way over to me, and I leaned in closer. It tipped forward, exposing the flat part of the arrow to me.

Not being able to resist, I lightly blew a warm breath of air across it, the leathery surface going from perfectly smooth to sprouting a hundred tiny goosebumps.

"Dane," Fern said breathlessly, smashing her face against my chest and pulling me closer.

I gently pressed my lips to it and gave it a little kiss, causing Fern to mew like a kitten. It might have been the sexiest sound I'd ever heard.

"Enough," she said, and stepped back.

"Aww. I was gonna lick it next."

Her eyes widened as she retreated a few more steps.

"I'm kidding!"

"Uh huh," she said sarcastically, eyes narrowed. "Keep it up, and I'll touch, kiss, and lick places you wouldn't appreciate."

"Um…"

She squawked and ran away, my bedroom door closing behind her.

CHAPTER 18

True to Danvers' word, the football team left me alone. A few even nodded at me in the hall. The cheerleaders were another story altogether. Snide comments, dirty looks, and even a sardine shoved through the vent in my locker became the norm. Fern had to be restrained at one point before lunch.

"I'm going to rip them to shreds," she hissed as I hugged her close.

"That probably shouldn't be said too loudly right now," I whispered softly.

That calmed her down. She exhaled slowly and pulled away, giving me an understanding nod.

"Come on, let's go to lunch."

"Okay."

We headed to the cafeteria, neither one of us talking. For the first time, I paid attention to what was going on around me, looking for trouble. I'd been blindsided too many times in the past.

Luckily, we made it to our usual spot in the center of the massive room without running into anyone in the baby blue, ruffled skirt, polyester-vest-wearing variety. If I never saw another pom-pom again, until the day I died, I'd be happy.

"I couldn't make a bento. Your mom doesn't have the right things."

"That's okay. I'm not really that hungry, anyway."

"I made lunch, just not the usual."

She pulled out two brown paper lunch bags and set one of them in front of me. Questioningly, I cocked an eyebrow at it before unrolling the end and looking inside. Two sandwiches in plastic baggies, a bag of chips, and a can of Coke were inside. Mom, not knowing what to buy, had bought standard mom fare. Seeing the carefully prepped basic lunch, my stomach growled.

"Thought you weren't hungry."

"I wasn't. Until I saw what you made."

"Do you not like the bento?"

"Yes, but every day… Change is nice every *once* in a while."

"Your mom helped me make the sandwiches. I'd never really done it before."

"What kind?"

"Peanut butter and jelly?"

"Sounds perfect," I said, and kissed her on the cheek.

One of the geekier kids of the school walked up with a tray of cafeteria food. My heart went out to him; I hoped he survived the experience. "Sorry to bother you, but would you mind if I sat here?"

I blinked in surprise. The kid standing in front of us was a geek. He was like twenty rungs up the social ladder from Fern and me. *We* were persona non grata. Outcasts. Lepers. "Uh, sure?"

He smiled eagerly and sat down, opening his drink. "I'm Michael, by the way."

"I'm Dane, and this is Fern."

He looked at me like Mt. Vesuvius had erupted from my forehead. "Yeah. I know. Everybody knows."

"I don't know if you know this, or care, but you do realize you are committing social suicide by sitting here, right?"

He chuckled, but then gave me a confused look. "You're kidding, right?"

"No?"

"You're like heroes. Both of you. To everyone who isn't on the cheerleading squad or football team."

I shot Fern a glance; she was just as confused as I was. I opened my mouth to ask why when another kid sat next to him. Then another. And another. A few minutes later, our once empty table was filled to capacity. It was like a scene out of an 80's movie. We were just missing an epic soundtrack playing in the background.

"So, is it true?"

I turned to the kid sitting next to Michael. "What?"

"You two live together?"

I almost spit peanut butter and jelly on him. "Where did you hear that?"

"I overheard the football players in the locker room during PE."

"They were talking about us?"

"Yeah. Apparently, Danvers had sent a group text about you last night, saying how you couldn't have let that thing into Trevor's house, how you lived together with your mom, and how Valerie was a lying piece of shit. They're not happy."

"They don't like being played," I said quoting the late, great Danvers.

"Yep. I'm Jason, by the way."

"Hi, Jason," Fern said shyly. I just nodded at him, still in a little shock.

"Well, if it isn't the Douchie Duo and the Nerd Herders."

I looked over my shoulder. Valerie and a couple of the cheerleaders stood directly behind us. "Hey, Skank Squad."

The entire table erupted in snickers. Valerie's face darkened, and I could almost feel the evil wafting from her. "Die, little man."

The snickering stopped. Everything stopped. She had said it loud enough that most of the cafeteria had heard her.

"Was that a threat?"

I *felt* the chill in Fern's voice.

"No. Just life advice," Valerie said, equally as chilly.

Fern picked up her can of Coke and opened it. To anybody not watching her every minute movement, they would have just seen

a pretty girl opening a can of Coke. I was waiting for her to shove the can into Valerie's chest or neck. I made it to mid-gasp of horror when she just popped the top. My eyes saw her *other* hand crush the can at the same moment, aiming it over her shoulder...

The force of the blast actually knocked Valerie back a step before she started yelling and sputtering, "You bitch! Don't tell me you didn't do that on purpose!"

"I just opened the can? I must have dropped it earlier and not noticed. I'm sorry. Here, have a napkin." She pulled a napkin off Jason's tray and held it over her head, not deigning to look at Valerie.

"What is going on here?" Principal Edwards stormed over to the table.

"Lucy's drink exploded, sir. Unfortunately, it landed on Valerie."

He probably wouldn't have believed me if every single person sitting down at our table didn't immediately start nodding in agreement. There was truth to the strength in numbers theory.

"Go get cleaned up, Miss Jones." His tone left little room for argument and firmly, yet politely, told her not to start any shit.

She harrumphed and stomped off, her mini-squad running after her. "Glad to see you both back at school," he said, and patted me on the shoulder before wandering around the lunch room.

"That's the first time I've ever seen him supervise lunch. Usually it's Dean Winchester," Michael said absentmindedly, watching the principal's retreating back.

"Winchester is off until next week, I heard. Some conference or something," Jason told him. "Get used to seeing him in here."

I glanced across the lunchroom and saw Valerie sitting at her table, glaring daggers at us. I smiled and waved. She gave me the finger. The rest of her table turned around, and I took that as my cue to concentrate on my sandwich.

Don't antagonize her. You might find a bear in your room. The nagging thought bore its way into my brain. I looked back up at her, and she was snarling something to the blonde cheerleader next to her. I had zero difficulty imagining Valerie with claws, horns, and wings.

She couldn't be. Could she? Why would she kill her boyfriend? To frame me? Seems a little doubtful. Maybe he was going to break up with her? Makes a little more sense. He found out what she was? That makes a lot more sense.

Either way, it was worth looking into. If anybody in the entire school was a murderous demon, it *had* to be Valerie Jones. Nobody else had the personality.

"Valerie, or the lunch lady stocking up on hamburger meat for sloppy joe day," I whispered to myself, lost in thought.

"What?"

"Nothing. I'll tell you later," I told Fern and gave her a quick peanut-butter-and-jelly-flavored kiss.

"Knock it off, Mr. Evans."

I looked behind me to see Principal Edward's glare at our public display of affection. "Sorry, sir."

Lunch ended, and everyone scattered to their next class. The rest of the day ended peacefully, at least. No sign of cheerleaders anywhere. I counted my blessings.

My phone buzzed in my pocket. Reaching down, I pulled it out and saw my mother had texted. I swiped open the text.

Going out with Brian tonight. You and Fern are on your own. There's TV dinners in the freezer. Love you.

PS. Behave.

I was chuckling when Fern latched on to my arm. "What?"

"Mom is going out with the detective tonight. She's got a date."

"Is that okay?"

"Of course. She deserves to be happy and the detective seems like a nice guy."

"Accidentally set fire to Santa's Village. He's not so nice."

"You need to tell me that story sometime."

"Meh. It really was an accident. I didn't know hairspray and that fake snow were so flammable. At least I got it."

"What?"

"The spider."

I shook my head slowly, stifling my laughter. "You're awesome."

"Huh?"

"Nothing. That was just the most Fern-like conversation I could ever imagine having with you."

"Is that good?"

"Better. So, what do you want to do? Do you want to go on a date with me?"

She nodded excitedly.

"Would you like to have dinner at the food court of the mall and wander around?"

She gave me a suspicious glance.

"I'll step on any spiders."

She nodded emphatically again.

"Okay then, it's a date. Let's go."

I stuffed my books in my locker. Friday had finally come around, and I wouldn't need them over the weekend anyway. I grabbed her hand and headed out the front door, anxious to spend some time with my girlfriend somewhere other than my house or school. I wondered what movies were playing at the theater. I had about a hundred dollars in my bank account. We were going to have a nice night for once.

We watched the endless stream of cars pour out of the parking lot. A pang of jealousy reared its ugly head. I wanted a car. Life would be so much easier if I wasn't reduced to walking everywhere like some sort of animal.

By the time we reached the mall, we were tired, cold, and hungry. Or, at least I was. Fern looked like she could run a marathon. Damn demon. I would have bet she wasn't even hungry. Until I heard her stomach growl. I smiled and thanked her human half in my head.

"Want to eat first?"

She nodded, eyes brightening and a cute, little smile crossing her face. "Yes!"

"What do you want to eat? I don't even know what they have."

"Chicken sandwiches."

"Chick-Fil-A?"

"Yes! They are so good."

I laughed, knowing what she meant. They were a favorite of mine, too. We even drove thirty minutes to get it in Chicago. "Chicken sandwiches, it is."

We made it to the food court and got in line for our food. The place was a well-oiled machine. Even a line of twenty people was no match for the horde of precisely trained teenagers manning the counters. We had our food and were sitting down within seven minutes.

I handed Fern her four sandwiches and twenty packs of mayo. She was sucking on her lemonade already. She had said no to fries, but I ordered for me. I knew how that would end...

"So, what were you going to tell me in the lunchroom earlier and said to wait until later? I think this qualifies as later."

Surprisingly enough, I understood every word, even with a mouthful of chicken sandwich, a slight pause, and another mouthful of chicken sandwich. I just didn't know what she was talking about. "Huh?"

"When you were looking at Valerie, and she gave you the finger. You looked like you thought of something."

"Oh. I *really* think she might be the demon."

"I thought you said she wasn't? How could she kill her own boyfriend?"

"I thought of three possibilities. One to frame me, but that seems kind of far to go. Extreme even. The second thought I had was that he was going to break up with her? Maybe she flipped out. The only other thing I can think of is that he found out she *is* a demon and killed him to keep her secret safe."

"That's one sick bitch, if she is the demon."

"What do you think?"

"Remember what I said? Demons are scary and impressive? They are this force of nature. They scare the shit out of me, and I'm *half* demon."

The couple at the table next to us gave Fern a strange look. She didn't bat an eyelash. "We're rehearsing a play," I lied, and turned my attention back to Fern. "But that was your father. All fathers are impressive and scary."

"Huh?"

"Fathers are scary."

"I never met my father. He knocked my mother up, and before she could even tell him, poof. Gone."

"Oh. I'm sorry. When you said you met a full demon, I thought you meant him."

162

"No. I meant someone else."

"Who? If you don't mind my asking."

"Detective James."

I spit chicken. Fern wiped off her hair and looked at me like I'd lost my mind. "Sorry!" I handed her a wad of napkins. "What the hell do you mean Detective James? My *mother* is dating a demon?"

"Excuse me, what's the name of this play? Is it going to be at the high school?"

I turned my head comically slow to the woman at the table next to us. "Um. It's a YMCA production of My Daddy's a Demon. I don't know if it's going to hit the stage, though. Kind of controversial, and we're still writing the script."

"Oh, I hope it does. Sounds quite interesting."

"That's my life," I said, gave her a small smile, and turned back to Fern. "He's a full-blooded demon?"

"Yeah. I found out when I got arrested. He yelled at me for getting in trouble. Said people were going to find out what I was."

"I thought you said scary and intimidating? He *could* be scary. I'll give you that. But, he's a nice guy?"

"Have him go full demon for you. You'll shit your pants."

"Is it safe for him to be dating my mother?"

"Demons are like people, Dane. You have good ones, and you have bad ones. There are more human monsters than real ones."

"True story."

"If you have a problem with him dating your mother, I would suggest you talk to him."

"That would be a bit hypocritical of me," I said with a wink.

She giggled. "Good. I thought it was kind of racist of you, too. But I didn't want to say anything."

"Always speak your mind. If I offend you or hurt your feelings, I damn well want to know."

She nodded.

"Wait. He has a sister. We met her at the restaurant."

"Yes. Demons do breed, you know."

And that's the moment I felt like the biggest dumbass on the planet. I took another bite of my food and reached for my fries. They were gone. So were all four of her sandwiches. She was even shaking her cup of ice.

"You ate my fries."

"You were too slow. I was helping."

"I wish I had *your* metabolism."

"Yeah, but the downsides outweigh the upsides."

"Out of curiosity, how long do demons live?"

"Forever."

CHAPTER 19

We laughed and held hands as we climbed the steps to the house. There weren't any cars in the driveway, so I assumed Mom was still on her date. Demon or not, I hoped she was having a good time. However, if he ever hurt her, physically or emotionally, I'd dump a thousand gallons of holy water on him. If that even worked.

I used my key to open the door and turned on all the lights before locking it back up. *Keep the door locked, you don't know what kind of crazy people are out there,* was one of her favorite sayings in the motherverse.

"Want to watch a movie?" I asked Fern. "We do have the house to ourselves…"

"Oh. Okay. I was going to suggest rolling around on the bed and touching each other inappropriately, but a movie sounds good, too." She laughed as my jaw hit the floor.

Not giving me a chance to change my mind, she plopped down on the couch. I joined her and grabbed the remote. We flipped through the channels and finally settled on a zombie movie.

Fern had her head on my shoulder when Mom and the detective opened the front door giggling like a couple of high school kids. "Glad to see you have her home before her curfew," I said to the detective.

He smiled and nodded, glancing up at the movie on the TV. "Saw this one. Everybody dies."

"Everybody is already dead. They're zombies."

"Oh. Thought this was Titanic."

"Don't get out much, do you Detective?"

"No. Work, home, and food."

"Shouldn't you kids be in bed?"

"Friday, Mom."

"Shouldn't you kids be in bed?"

"Oh, would you and the detective like our seats?"

"That is so sweet of you," she said mockingly. "Coffee, Brian?"

"Yes, please."

"Well, we'll be off to bed. Come on, Fern. We can watch this on my tablet."

I stood and held out my hand to help her up. She reached out with a hand sporting inch-long talons, and clutched mine. In a panic, I looked up at Mom, but she was busy in the kitchen making coffee.

"Fern, *hand*," I hissed. I didn't care if the detective saw, for obvious reasons. Mom would freak.

The detective casually tossed his jacket over our joined hands. "Hang that up for me, would you?"

"Sure thing, Detective," I said, and nodded my thanks. "Come on, Fern."

She had a glazed look in her eyes and didn't seem all there. Two bumps had formed on her forehead that hadn't quite poked through her skin yet.

The detective leaned over and whispered, "And feed her."

"Feed her?"

"You know. Bow chika wow wow. Go."

I nodded, hoisting Fern to her feet and helping her toward the bedroom.

"Just toss my jacket on that chair over there. No need to hang it up."

166

"Okay," I said, grateful for his quick thinking. I pulled it off Fern's hands and set it down as we walked by the recliner.

"Night, kids," Mom called out from the kitchen.

"Night, Mom. Have fun. Night, Detective."

He just nodded and sighed.

I got Fern into bed. The detective's comment kind of freaked me out, honestly. But at the same time, made a lot of sense. Every time she had gotten sick, we had fooled around and miraculously, she was cured.

Maybe she's some kind of sex demon? A succubus?

I should have been happier than I was with that realization. Instead, I was just worried. "Fern? What can I do to help?"

"Hold me."

I lay down next to her and pulled her into my arms "Whatever you need, sweetie."

She started by kissing my neck and rubbing my chest while I held her tight. Her panting became louder and louder. I could feel her rubbing her entire body against me.

"Touch me," she whispered.

I rolled on my side, and she nestled in closer to me, her lips inches from mine. I closed the distance between them and gently sucked her bottom lip into my mouth, grazing it with my teeth. She pulled back and attacked me with her kiss, her tongue finding its way into my mouth and running over the front of my teeth.

My hand slid down her shoulder, over her arm and onto her ass. I pulled her into me, and we were pressed together from chest to knees, the heat building between us. "Take off your pants."

"Fern…"

"You said *whatever I need.* I need you."

The bathroom had broken down all the last barriers between us. We were no longer strangers to each other's bodies. I just didn't know if I could do anything like that with my mother in the living room…

"Hurry…"

I slid my hand off her and in between us, unbuckling my belt and jeans with one hand and pushing them down. She kicked off her leggings much the same way. There we lay on the bed, with no barriers between us.

She crawled on top of me, reached over and shut off the light. The only illumination in the room was the heat in her eyes.

It made the sensation of what followed all the more real.

∞ ∞ ∞

I woke up, drained. In more ways than one. My mouth was dry, and I had a bit of a headache. Fern was passed out in my arms. I couldn't see her, but I could feel the contentment radiating from her. I kissed the back of her head and slid my arm out from beneath her.

She woke up and stretched lazily, rolling on her back. "You okay?"

"Yes, but my head hurts a little. I'm going to go get some water and Advil. Need anything?"

"You. Hurry back."

"I will," I said with a chuckle, and gently kissed her lips as I ran my fingers over her stomach.

The light was on in the living room, but nobody was out there, and the TV was off. Mom must have gone to bed and the detective home. She was off on the weekends, so I was a little surprised they weren't still up. I shrugged and headed for the kitchen and the sweet promise of getting rid of my headache.

I had grabbed a bottle of water from the fridge and popped two Ibuprofen from the bottle, when Mom's door opened and closed. She was probably checking on me. I waited by the kitchen door to scare her when the detective rounded the corner. I was glad I saw it was him before I said, "Boo."

"Hey," he said when he saw me.

I was shocked he was spending the night. But again, that was kind of hypocritical of me, too. "Evening, Detective," I said with a little smile.

"What are you doing up?"

"Headache," I said, and shook the bottle of pills on the counter.

He nodded. "That happens. She okay?"

"Yeah," I said guiltily.

"You knew?"

"About Fern? Or you?"

"Both."

"Yes. I saw her coming out of the shower one night wearing a towel. She can't hide her wings, and the towel didn't hide much, either."

"That was careless. You're not supposed to know about us."

"Yeah. It wasn't her fault. I just happened to get up."

He let it go. "She told you about me?"

"Yeah. We were discussing the murders. It's a demon doing it. She's sure of it. She could feel it when the two guys were murdered."

He sighed. "I know. Come and sit. This is going to be a long conversation. Want a Coke? Caffeine will help."

He made a cup of coffee while I grabbed a can out of the fridge. I waited for the hissing and bubbling to stop. Luckily, the single serve maker was quick. We headed into the dining room and sat, without turning on the light. We could see well enough from the light in the living room. Hell, for all I knew, he could see in the dark.

"First thing I've got to say is, you're handling all this quite well."

"The demon thing?"

"Yeah."

"Well, Fern is everything I could ever hope for in a girlfriend. Fun. Funny. Beautiful. I wasn't lying when I told her I love her."

"Just be careful. She's not fully human and could hurt you on accident."

"She couldn't hurt a fly. If I get hurt, it would probably be from doing something stupid. I'm a cautious individual at heart."

"I see that. Now my next question is about me. Do you have a problem with me dating your mother?"

"That would be hypocritical."

"Most humans are."

"True. And I'll admit, I *am* worried about you hurting her."

"I would never…"

"I mean emotionally. Divorce, her ex dying. She's the strongest woman I've ever seen in my short life, but she hasn't had the best luck with men. And you're a cop. Do you have any idea the divorce rate of police officers?"

"You're more worried about me being a cop than a demon?"

I nodded. "Just like I'm more worried about you breaking her heart than shredding her flesh with your inch-long talons."

"I take it Fern hasn't told you what a full demon looks like?"

"She said I would shit my pants and left it at that."

"Well, I'm not going to show you tonight, but I will. You can judge for yourself. Let's just say Fern is like a kitten, and I'm a lion."

"Oh."

"Yeah. We call them half-demons, but the ratio is more skewed than that. Humanity is a lot stronger than most of us would like to admit. My talons are a hell of a lot longer than an inch. It's why I didn't suspect Fern of killing those boys. She could kill them, but you didn't see the damage they took."

"So, do you feed like Fern? Should I leave the Advil out for Mom?"

He chuckled. "No. There are *many* types of demons. Some have affinity for different elements. Some feed on different things. Some on fear, some on hope, and some even on love. Many divorces happen because the love is gone, eaten by a demon who got too close to the couple."

"Is that what Fern is? Is she feeding on my love for her?"

"No. You see, kid, all half-demons are the same. Their true name is succubae. They feed on lust and sex."

"So that's why you said bow chicka wow wow when you told me to feed her."

"Yep. You don't actually have to do the nasty, and I'm sure your mother would appreciate that. You just have to *want* her. She can feed on that."

"But not as well."

"You sound like you're speaking from experience."

"I am. And until a week or so ago, I was totally inexperienced."

"And now?"

I shrugged, not really comfortable talking about it.

"That was answer enough."

"Do succubae live forever like full-demons?"

"Depends. Eventually, even the most dour and jaded of them eventually fall in love with a human. Once their mate dies, they fade away."

"If I die, she dies?"

"If your bond is strong enough, yes."

"That sucks."

He shrugged. "Not always. Sometimes, immortality isn't the greatest gift…"

171

"How old are you and your sister?"

"I'm nearly six-hundred. My sister, four."

"Wow. Bet you've seen some shit."

"You have no idea. But I like this modern world. It's why I became a cop. Keep it a little safer for the good people."

His answer shocked me. Given limitless power and immortality, I wasn't quite sure what I would do with eternity. With my distrust and general dislike of people, I think I would just sit back with a bucket of popcorn and watch the shit show. "You're an interesting person, Detective."

"Brian. Call me, Brian. Please. The detective shit gets old."

I laughed and nodded.

"You're an interesting kid, Dane."

"Well, I have an awesome mom."

"That you do. And I promise not to break her heart or shred her."

"Thanks."

"No problem."

"So, what do we do about this demon killing kids at my school?"

"*We* do nothing. I will handle it. Just try not to piss anybody off at school. That doesn't seem to be good for their health."

"I know, right? That's why I think it's Valerie. I've been pissed at her since the moment I met her. She's still kicking, though."

"The first victim's girlfriend?"

"Yeah. The one who told everybody I was at his house. I told you about that."

"Maybe. I'll have to interview her again. I wasn't looking for the signs."

"Signs?"

"I'll tell you about what to look for, someday. It's late, and it would take way too long."

"One last question, if a human and a half-demon have kids, what would they be like?"

"No superficial traits. Exceptional skills and talent. Da Vinci. Einstein. A lot of actors and politicians."

"Woah."

"You're not planning on…"

"No! I was just wondering what kind of future Fern and I had together."

"A long one, hopefully."

"I just don't know if I could be responsible for her losing her immortality. How could I live with that?"

"You already have. You two are bonded. So, don't die."

"Are you going to tell Mom?"

"If we spend a decade together, she'll figure it out on her own. Until then…"

"I can see that. Be good to her. She deserves it."

He rapped his knuckles on the table and chugged his coffee. "*That*, I *can* do. Night, kid."

"Night, Brian."

CHAPTER 20

Fern's ringing phone woke me up from my much needed sleep. I glanced at the clock on the nightstand. It wasn't even eight in the morning. Who the hell calls someone before eight in the morning on a *Saturday*?

I sat up in shock. It was the first time anybody had *ever* called her that I could recall.

I shook her shoulder. "Fern. Your phone."

She blinked lazily and focused on my face, tilting her head toward her blaring ringtone. She had put her phone on my desk.

She slid out from under the covers, still not wearing anything below her T-shirt, and crossed the room. I raised my eyebrows and smiled at her naked butt. I don't think I could ever get tired of seeing that.

"Hello?"

The moment she saw who was calling, her face went dead, and it didn't change until she spoke. "No."

Her blank expression morphed as she began chewing worriedly on her thumbnail. A tear rolled down her cheek, fell, and soaked into her white shirt.

"I can't. I really can't."

She shut the phone off and put it back on the desk, turning to face the wall as she cried. I got right up out of bed and ran across the room, throwing my arms around her.

She turned and sobbed into my chest.

"What is it?"

She shook her head. "Nothing."

I could have said a hundred things. I could have told her it didn't sound like nothing. I could have asked if she was okay. Instead, I gave her some privacy. "Okay."

She blinked up at me, kind of surprised. "Okay?"

"Yes. If you want to tell me, you will. I'm not going to pry if you don't want to talk about it."

"I do. But I want you to pry it out of me and tell me what to do."

I laughed. Women should come with an instruction manual. Fern should have come with two. "Do you want to talk about it now? Do you want to go back to bed for a little bit? Or do you want me to make you some coffee?"

"Coffee, talk, bed. That order."

"Okay. Come on."

Taking her hand, I pulled her from the room, setting her down on the couch and going into the kitchen, putting a cup on to brew. I glanced at Mom's door, wondering if the detective was still over or if he had gone home.

Finally, the coffee finished, and I grabbed the mug, heading back into the living room. I set it down on the table in front of her and sat on the other end of the couch, turning to face her and putting my feet on the cushion between us.

She picked up her coffee and did the same.

"Um... Fern."

"What?"

"If you're going to sit like that, please go put something on."

She smiled at me wickedly and opened her legs for a fraction of a second, before tucking them underneath her and pulling her shirt over her legs. It was too late. The damage had been done. I shifted my position to hide my parts.

"Sorry. I needed the distraction."

"It worked," I answered, and raised my eyebrows.

"I like that I have that effect on you."

"Me, too. Now talk. Who was that on the phone?"

"The psychiatric hospital."

"Your mom okay?"

She cocked an eyebrow at me.

"Is your mother in any danger?" I rephrased my question.

"No. She's lucid today. She told the doctor she would like to see me. They called to see if I would come down."

"Do you want to go?"

She shook her head.

"Are you going to go?"

She shrugged.

"Are you going to go, and want me to go with you?"

She nodded slowly.

"Mom is off today. I can see if she'll take us."

"I don't want your mother…"

"She already knows. She won't go inside with us, if that's what you're worried about."

"We could take the bus…"

"Does it go that way?"

She nodded again.

"Would you prefer to do that?"

She nodded slowly.

"You're making this rather difficult."

"I'm sorry," she said, and took a sip of her coffee. "I get a little weird when it comes to my mother."

"Fern, sweetie. I don't know how to tell you this…"

"Oh, God. You're going to break up with me?"

"What? No. Jesus. What the hell? I'd never break up with you. Where did that come from?"

"You're worried I'm going to turn into my mother…"

"You're a lot weird. That's what I was going to say. I was making a joke to make you smile. No, I don't think you're going to turn into your mother. I don't think that's possible, but I think *you're* worried you will. Your mother couldn't handle what you are. It broke her. It's not your fault, and it's not really hers, either. I blame your father. Things might have been a lot different if he had just stuck around, the same with mine. Stop blaming yourself, and stop worrying, okay?"

"Sure. Seventeen years of anxiety gone just like that." She snapped her fingers. "Thanks."

"You're welcome!" I smiled, not getting drawn into her trap.

"That was sarcasm."

"Yep. I'm proud of you."

"You're impossible."

"No. I'm being supportive. I know you're terrified of seeing her, but I'll be there with you. My turn to protect you."

Another tear slid down her cheek. She set her coffee down and crawled over to kiss me, lying her head in my lap after and stretching out on the couch. She even pulled her shirt over her butt in case my mother came out of her room. Which she did.

She took one look at us and gave me a questioning stare.
"What?"

"What the hell are you doing up already? And don't think I didn't notice you slept in the same room last night. Do I need to put up trip wires?"

The detective walked out of her room and slapped her on the butt. "Pot, kettle." He laughed and headed into the kitchen.

"You stay out of this!"

He ignored her and started making coffee.

She sighed and said to the ceiling, "How did my life turn out like this?"

"Mom," I said, interrupting her pleas. "The hospital called; Fern's mom wants to see her. We're going down there later."

"Oh. Oh! Are you okay, sweetie?"

Fern nodded on my chest, not elaborating.

"We're going to take the bus."

"Take the car. I'm not going anywhere today."

"You sure?" I was shocked. I had my license, but she *never* let me take the car.

"It was going to be a surprise, but it's yours. Brian's taking me to buy another used one today. Now that money won't be so tight, I figured we should have something a little more reliable. You need a car. The catch is, you need to get a job to pay for gas and insurance."

"Deal!"

"And you need to get your Virginia license, ASAP. Got it?"

"Yes, ma'am."

"See, Brian? Disrespectful little shit gets all respectful when you give him a car."

"Ingrate," he said, pulling one mug out and putting the other in the coffee maker, swapping pods and hitting the start button.

Mom sat down on the recliner and looked everywhere but at Fern, whose derriere was pointed at Mom. Hopefully, she couldn't see anything, or her lack of anything. We needed to get up before Brian came in.

"Well, we're going back to bed for a bit. This is way too early."

Mom shot me a look that withered my soul.

Yep. She saw.

"Come on, Fern."

She crawled off me and got to her feet. I pressed a hand to her lower back to usher her away to safety…

179

Parking was spacious at the Oak Hills Psychiatric Hospital. There were like ten cars in the parking lot, and ours was one of the nicer ones.

Fern looked like a zombie as she popped the door open, got out, and started walking slowly toward the entrance. I could see dread in every one of her movements. I didn't even need to hurry to catch up to her. Instead of offering her encouraging words, I tucked her hand in mine, squeezing it softly.

"You sure you want to come in with me?"

"Absolutely. I can't promise you much, but I can promise you this... You will never have to do this alone again."

She let go of my hand and buried her face in my chest. I kissed the top of her head and rocked her in the middle of the parking lot.

"Thank you."

"No need. I love you."

"I love you, too."

She let go and headed for the door again, this time a little more animatedly. I grabbed the handle, pulling it open for her. She marched up to the desk.

It took a moment for the orderly to finish writing whatever he was writing on the clipboard in front of him.

"I'm here to see Deborah Fern? Doctor Angelo called me."

"You must be Lucy. Hang on, I'll page the doctor."

We sat on the plastic benches by the front door. The large fake, plastic tree next to me didn't have a spot of dust on it. The place seemed clean and well-maintained. Even the linoleum floor gleamed brightly under the fluorescent lights above.

The only thing that bothered my senses was the underlying smell of stale something. The place was heavily sanitized, but it wasn't strong enough to mask the smell of urine and other things I'd rather not think about.

The door leading into the hospital buzzed, and a tall, tired-looking, balding doctor stepped out in a lab coat. "You came," he said to Fern, surprised.

Fern nodded and stood. I took my place behind her.

"Come on back. I'm sure Debbie will be happy to see you."

"I doubt that."

"To be honest, I'd say it's fifty-fifty. She's more lucid today than she's been since she was admitted, but her mood shifts frequently and quickly. If you get uncomfortable, leave the room."

Fern looked even more nervous, if that was possible.

"I wouldn't recommend bringing your friend…"

I was prepared to sit down. I even started to when Fern spun and grabbed my arm, shaking her head. She turned back to the doctor. "This is my boyfriend. I didn't want to do this, but he came with me to help me get through it. If he can't go, I don't go."

The doctor nodded in understanding. "Okay. I would let her know you brought somebody with you before he goes into the room, though."

"Okay."

"If it's a problem I can step out of the room and be right outside for you," I told her.

She shook her head adamantly.

The doctor led us down the main corridor and then down another smaller hallway. The room at the end had a glass viewing window with wire mesh embedded into it. He peered inside, nodded, and unlocked the door from the outside.

My impression of psychiatric wards had always been patients in a group environment, sitting around card tables playing checkers and watching movies while their meds kept them docile. This situation spoke volumes on Debbie's condition.

The door swung open and the doc walked in, motioning for us to wait. "Debbie? Lucy is here to see you. She brought a friend with her. Is that okay?"

"Lucy? My little Lucy? Wings spread, send her in. Spawn of Satan."

I could feel Fern's back tighten in apprehension. I ran my fingers over her arm. "I'm here," I whispered.

She leaned back and pressed herself against me while waiting for the doctor to invite us in. He popped his head out and said, "Come in, slowly."

Fern shuffled forward. When she crossed the threshold, I followed her. The walls of the room were padded, just like you'd expect from the movies. The only furniture in the room was the small white nightstand with metal legs bolted to the floor and the heavily padded bed that Debbie was strapped to. Scars crisscrossed her arms and neck, thin lines. Debbie had tried to kill herself, repeatedly. I gulped as the gravity of her illness truly struck home.

"Hi, my Lucy. Mommy's home."

"Hello, Mother."

"Who is that boy with you. Is he human?"

Fern sighed. "Yes, Mother. This is my boyfriend, Dane."

"Hello, Dane. Sorry if I can't get up. I'm very tired today. Can't seem to drag my bones out of bed."

"Hello," I said softly.

"Oh, you seem like a nice boy. Do you know what my daughter is?"

I glanced over at the doctor, his attention was focused on his patient. Not me. I turned and looked at Debbie and nodded.

"Spawn of the devil," she sang softly from her bed.

"How are you feeling, mother?"

"Like a bastard demon crawled from my guts and threw me into hell. How 'bout you?"

"I'm well. School is good. I've moved in with Dane and his mother."

"Slut."

"They're taking care of me now. Aunt Sarah left."

"Chicken shit Sarah. Can't take care of my baby demon. Demon. Demon."

"Well, I just wanted to let you know that everything is fine with me. You should rest and get better soon."

"Okay. I'll do that. What's that smell? Do you smell that?" She sat up an inch, the limit of her restraints. She started frantically sniffing the air. "I can smell him. He's here."

"Who's here, Debbie?" The doctor stepped forward and placed his fingers on her wrist, checking her pulse.

"The damned demon who put that abomination in my belly. I can smell him. You can't smell him? Oh, God. I need to shower. Help me find my pretty dress."

"There's nobody here, Debbie. I need you to relax." He motioned for us to wait out in the hall."

"See, Debbie? There's nobody here but you and me."

"No, Doc. He's here. I can smell him, taste him. He's in my head."

"Well, you should get some sleep. I'll be back to check on you later."

The doctor stepped back out into the hall, shaking his head sadly and locking the door behind him. He motioned to the way we had come and fell into step next to Fern. "That didn't go as well as I'd hoped."

"I can't believe you expected anything else. It's the same thing every time I come here, Doctor. Please don't ask me again. You have no idea what that woman did to me." Fern sounded angrier than I'd ever heard her.

"I don't know because you won't tell me. We really need to talk about it sometime."

"No, thank you. I'd rather not relive the memories." She stomped off ahead of us by a couple of paces.

"I thought you said she was lucid," I said to the doctor.

"She was. We were having normal conversations this morning. That's when she asked to see Lucy. She said she wanted to say goodbye to her and let her live her life."

"What?"

"Yeah. I think she wanted to tell Lucy not to worry about her anymore. I took it as a sign of her getting better. But, as soon as she saw her daughter, she fell right back into her demonic delusion."

"Well, you did the best you could, Doc. Good luck," I said, and jogged to catch up to Fern

"Could you hear all that," I whispered

"Yes."

"Good. I'm sorry, Fern."

She grabbed my hand and held it tightly. Almost too tightly. It was starting to hurt, but I let her do it anyway. "Thank you. Thank you for not making me do that alone."

"You're welcome."

CHAPTER 21

The back seat of Mom's new SUV was pretty comfortable. Fern and I had plenty of room, and we were sort of leaning toward each other to hold hands. Mom was driving us to a Japanese steakhouse someone had told her about at work. The detective sat in the passenger seat. It almost felt like a family dinner.

I should have known it wouldn't go well.

Fern's phone and the detective's phone went off almost at the same moment. Fern got hers out first, frowned, and answered it. She was staring at the back of Mom's headrest as the color drained from her face. Fern was naturally pale, but she went almost ghostly.

"Detective James," he answered his phone. "I'll be there in thirty."

He turned to face Fern and then stared at his phone for a second. "Stop the car, Connie."

Mom shot him a questioning glance, and he just looked at her. Her eyes saw Fern in the rearview mirror, and her face took on that worried look mothers all seemed to instinctively share.

"What's going on?" She pulled into a drugstore parking lot.

Fern was still on the phone, but not really saying anything. I had a feeling I knew, but I wanted to make sure.

Finally, she hung up, turned to me with doe-like eyes and burst into sobs.

Unbuckling my seatbelt, I slid across the leather seats and pulled her into my arms.

"What's going on?" Mom reiterated again, this time almost frantically.

"There was a murder at the Oak Hills Psychiatric Ward," the detective told her solemnly.

"Fern?"

He nodded.

"Oh, God no."

"I need to get over there. The doctor wants to talk to me."

"I assume you want to go then, too?" He turned almost all the way around to see me.

I looked at Fern in my arms. "Yes."

"Do you mind driving, Connie?"

"Just tell me where."

It took us less than thirty minutes to get there. Mom parked in the space closest to the entrance. "Should I come in?"

"Probably not a good idea. I'll send the kids out to you as soon as they're done with the doctor."

"Okay. I have a book on my phone, so take your time."

He smiled, leaned over, and kissed her.

Fern gave me a scared look. I got out of the car, walked around, opened the door for her, and offered my hand. She pulled herself out of the seat and pressed her head against me.

"Come on. You can do this."

She nodded, shook her head, and nodded again. I held her hand the entire way.

There were four cars parked around the entrance, blue lights flashing. Detective James held up his badge as he walked through them. We stayed close and walked right in behind him.

Doctor Angelo was sitting in the lobby, waiting for either us or the detective. I wasn't sure which. He finally looked up and saw Fern and made a beeline directly for her, ignoring everything and everyone else in the room.

"Lucy, I am so sorry."

She just nodded, and he ushered her through the door, not allowing me to follow.

"Doctor!"

He paused and turned to the detective.

"The girl is a minor. Having her sign anything won't hold up in court," he said cryptically.

Angelo's face slumped.

"What's going on, Brian?"

"He was probably planning on having Fern sign all sorts of denial of liability forms. Her mother was killed *in* the hospital. Their security should have prevented this. He's afraid of getting sued. Go with her, read everything she signs."

"Okay," I said, and walked over to them.

"If she's a minor, we're going to need a guardian to sign, too."

"I'll sign for her. After I'm done with the investigation."

"You're a family member?"

"As much as she has right now," the detective said, leaving little to no room for argument.

The doctor sighed again and ushered us into the hospital, then into his office. He motioned to the two chairs in front of his desk and moved to the large file cabinet on the far wall. Pulling keys off his ring, he unlocked the files and pulled a very large one out of the front, setting it on his desk.

"I'm going to officially discharge your mother, and I'll arrange to have her personal effects brought up."

"Personal effects?"

"Yes. Whatever they had on their person at time of admission. We keep the items downstairs in storage and give them back upon discharge. It's to help the patients move on with their lives as soon as they leave."

Sounded more like prison, but I guessed it made sense. Fern just nodded, poised to sign everything set in front of her. I don't think she even cared what it was.

I took everything he handed her, looked it over, and started two piles. One in front of her to sign and one questionable one, I wanted the detective to look at before she did.

"So how do you know the detective?"

Not wanting to tell him about the murders, I edited the events. "He's a friend of the family and is dating my mother."

"I see."

I said nothing else, not really trusting him after the detective's revelation.

Finally, she finished just as there was a knock at the door. The doctor got up and opened it. "Come in, Detective."

Brian strolled into the room. "How's it going?"

"Almost done. She signed the discharge papers and for her mother's personal effects. I wanted you to look these over before she signed." I handed him the relatively small stack of papers. The first two he set in front of Fern, the third he handed back to the doctor. After that, it turned into a one for her, one for you scenario, splitting the papers between them. One to sign, and one not to. The doctor didn't look happy about it but didn't say a single word in protest.

"Fern. I hate to ask. But could you come with me? I want you to identify the body, just for the record. Then you won't have to do it later. Not usually protocol, but I thought it might be easier on you."

I sort of doubted the validity of his reasoning, but he was six hundred years old. Maybe he was right.

Fern nodded and stood. I started to, but the detective stopped me. "You probably don't want to see."

Instead of answering, I looked at Fern. This wasn't about what I wanted. This was about what she needed. Panic was clearly written on her face. There was my answer. "Neither does Fern. We'll do it together," I answered, and saw her relax a fraction.

He nodded and led the way we had walked earlier that day.

I held Fern in my arms, letting her bury her head in my shoulder as we awkwardly walked down the halls. The petty part of me thought about how at least she would never have to go through this again. The loving side of me wished she had never had to do it to begin with.

The detective stopped in the doorway. "Could you clear the room and give us a few?"

Three crime scene investigators stepped out of the room.

Fern and I walked in, the detective shutting the door behind us. I saw the body, still strapped down to the bed. Her arms, her legs, and her head were the only things recognizable. I held Fern tightly in my arms, not letting her see. "Could you drape a sheet over her?"

Sadly, he shook his head. "They're not done. Can't disturb the crime scene."

Now, I was totally doubting his decision to have her identify the body.

Fern pulled away and turned, gasping at the sight of her mother's remains. She didn't cry. She didn't throw up. She just stared and seemed almost at peace. It creeped me out more than the sight of the body.

"She was happy," she whispered. "She wanted this."

Confused, I looked at her face. Even in death, she smiled. "She knew it was coming," I mumbled.

"What?"

I glanced up at the detective. "When we were here earlier, she told the doctor that she wanted to say goodbye to her daughter. He said he thought she wanted her to stop worrying about her. Now I'm not so sure. I think she knew her death was coming."

"Is that all she said?"

"No. She kept going on about how she could smell him. And she needed to get ready. Wear a pretty dress or something."

"Who's he?"

"The demon that put Fern in her belly. Fern's father…"

∞ ∞ ∞

"I'm half tempted to pack up our shit and move us all back to Chicago."

The detective nodded in the seat next to Mom. I watched their exchange from the back. Fern sat next to me with the box of her mother's personal things on her lap, staring out the window.

"That might not be a bad idea. I don't mean permanently, either… I'm too selfish for that. But why don't you and the kids go back for a mini-vacation?"

Mom nodded thoughtfully. "The kids probably shouldn't be missing any more school, though."

"Talk to the principal. Tell him you're doing it to keep them safe. He can't argue with that."

"Won't you miss me?"

"Every minute, but I'd rather you be seven hundred miles safer."

"Could you come with us?"

"I have a killer to catch, so you can come home."

"Dane?"

I looked at Fern before answering. She still wasn't paying attention. "Fern." I shook her leg.

"I'm not hungry," she said without turning.

"Would you like to go to Chicago with us? Get away from here for a while?"

She shrugged.

I squeezed her hand. She turned and looked at me, wiping some tears from her eyes as her lip quivered. "If you want to stay, we can," I said.

She shook her head. "No. Let's go."

I nodded. "We'll go."

The detective smiled, seemingly happy. He really was worried about Mom's safety. I liked that.

"I'll call Mom and Dad tonight," Mom told him.

"Wouldn't a nice hotel somewhere be nice?"

"You just know they'll make you sleep in separate rooms," she said with a small chuckle.

"Yeah. And it's Gramma and Grampa. Maybe a Motel 6? I'm not picky."

"We'll see."

Mom parked in front of the pizza place she called the order into, ran inside, and returned with two large pies she set on Brian's lap.

"That smells delicious."

She nodded at him. "One meatball and one sausage. It ain't Chicago style, but it will have to do."

I groaned, missing *real* pizza. I would have to take Fern out for some when we went. The more I thought about it, the more excited I got. I could show her where I grew up. I could show her what a real mall looked like. I could even take her up on top of the Willis Tower.

"You're going to love Chicago."

CHAPTER 22

"I can't go."

I stared at my mother in disbelief. "Why?"

"We're gearing up for the holiday season. I just couldn't get the time off."

"But you're the freaking store manager, Mom."

"Which is precisely why I can't. I'm sorry."

I was being selfish, I realized, but I'd fantasized about showing Fern everything I missed about Chicago. To not go now, was kind of heartbreaking. I think Fern realized; she rubbed my leg gently.

"Connie, can I talk to you for a minute?"

She nodded at Brian and followed him outside.

"What's that all about?" I wondered aloud.

"He's trying to convince her on the importance of leaving. She's arguing that she can't go. He understands that, and that wasn't what he was talking about. She's confused. Now he's bringing up the idea of letting you and I go off on our own, just until the killer is caught."

I snapped my fingers in front of her. She stopped her play-by-play reiteration of their conversation. "You can hear them?"

She nodded.

"Well, that's kind of awkward. You never listened to me in the shower, have you?"

She gave me an evil grin.

My cheeks felt like they were going too burst into flames.

"Don't worry. It was kind of hot. I joined you from my room. And your room. Once in the kitchen..."

"Oh, my God. Stop."

The front door opened again and the both of them walked in. Mom sat on the chair facing Fern and me. "I'm going to stay home. I want the two of you to take my car and go. You *will* be staying with Gramma and Grampa. I'll call and make the arrangements with them. It's only ten hours or so. I want you to be *careful*. This is not a vacation. I am doing this to keep the two of you safe. Do you understand?"

"Absolutely." I said the word as somberly as possible as I danced around in my head.

"Good. Go pack. I'll give you my gas card and my credit card. This is for meals and emergencies."

"Yes, ma'am."

She rolled her eyes. "Lord, help me. What the hell am I doing?" She stood and headed for her bedroom.

"Being a good mom!"

Brian watched the exchange from the kitchen. He winked at me when I looked at him.

"I love you, man," I whispered.

"Don't think I didn't hear you just wink at my son!" Mom's voice rang clearly from the bedroom.

The detective's eyes widened in shock. "She's scary."

"You have no idea. Come on, Fern. Let's go pack."

"Okay."

She followed me into my bedroom and gathered what she had left in there before heading into her room to stuff everything in a suitcase. I looked at my ratio of dirty to clean clothes and let out a sigh of disappointment.

Maybe I can talk Gramma into washing a couple of loads for me when we get there...

"Fern, if you have any dirty clothes you want to bring, give them to me. I'm taking some in a garbage bag."

A few minutes later, she walked in carrying some in her arms. I tried very hard not to stare at her panties as she tossed the pile on the corner of my bed. Without a word, she went back to her room to pack.

I went out to the kitchen to grab a garbage bag. Mom and Brian were in her room, and I could hear Mom still on the phone with the grandparents. She mentioned the words "killer," "mother," and "kids at school." She must have been telling them the whole story. As much as she knew, anyway.

I grabbed the bag and headed back to my room, scooping the pile of dirty clothes into the garbage bag and shoving the clean ones into my suitcase. The suitcase I'd used more in the past two weeks than I had in the past two years.

I just needed to pack my chargers and my laptop in case I needed it. And grab my toothbrush and rest of my toiletries. Other than that, I was set to go.

Brian surprised me by knocking softly on my doorframe, leaning against it when I turned around.

"Got a minute?"

"Sure. What's up?"

"I couldn't really say anything at the hospital, or with your mom around, but I definitely smelled a demon at the crime scene."

I dropped down on my bed, nodding at the detective. "Not surprised. You really think it was Fern's father?"

"Well, it definitely wasn't a cheerleader, so I think you can throw that theory out the window."

Nodding, I shrugged. "It would have been a little too convenient if it was Valerie. She's just a bitch. But why go after all the football players? They were targeting me, not Fern. And does this mean Fern's dad works at the school? Or is he just omnipresent?"

"No demon is omnipresent. We're just people. With fangs. We can be hurt, and we can be killed."

"How?"

He chuckled. "You worried I'm going to piss of your mother?"

"No! I can understand you not wanting to tell me, but just in case..."

He nodded. "I know. I was just joking. Steel and salt."

"What?"

"Those are the two things that can hurt a demon. Steel and salt." He winked and turned around, heading back toward my mother, who was still on the phone.

I headed for the living room, stopping by Fern's room to check on her. She was slowly and daintily folding her T-shirts and laying them neatly in her suitcase. I smiled at her and went to check on the other arrangements.

Mom finally got off the phone, and she and Brian hugged in her room. I decided to let them have their moment, plopping my ass down on the couch after I snagged a can of Coke from the fridge. Flipping on the TV, I started surfing through channels until I found a rerun of a cartoon I used to watch.

I stared absentmindedly, thinking about the places I wanted to take Fern and making a mental list. I wasn't exactly comfortable about driving into downtown, but the grandparents lived close enough to the train station that we could use that. It would even be cheaper than parking and gas. Probably.

Fern came out and plopped down next to me. I smiled and gave her a quick kiss. "You ready to go?"

"Yes. Do I have time to take a quick shower?"

"Yeah. We don't have a schedule. Knock yourself out."

"Okay. Want to come with me?"

"Yeah, right. I value my life."

She flashed me a wicked grin. "Want to borrow my super hearing?"

I groaned. The girl was literally going to kill me from blood draining from my brain into my lower extremities. "You said a quick shower…"

"Oh. It *will* be. There will be tail involved…"

"Fern!" I hissed, rolling my eyes and laying back in the couch. She'd done it. I was dead.

She laughed, kissed my dead lips, running her nails down my thigh as she got up and shook her ass all the way to the bathroom. Just before she shut the door, she pulled down her shorts, and her tail made its appearance. I was tempted to say, "Screw it," and jump off the couch. I didn't want my mother to kill me before we left, so I took deep, deep breaths.

"You all set to go?'

I looked over at Mom as she came out of her bedroom. "Yeah. Fern's taking a shower, but we're packed."

She sat down on the couch next to me and flopped her head over on my shoulder. "Please be careful. I can't lose you, kiddo."

"I know, Mom. I will. I promise."

"My fear of losing you is the only reason I'm allowing you two to go on this little excursion in the first place."

"I know."

"And there's something else I want to talk to you about."

"What?"

"Look. I know you two are…doing the nasty. *Please*, for the love of God, be careful. First of all, I'm too damn young to be a grandparent. Use my credit card and buy some protection, at least."

"Not how I thought this conversation was going to go, but okay."

"Secondly, *be respectful* while you are staying at your grandparents house. Tell Fern to wear multiple layers of clothing and *no hanky panky.*"

"Is that what the cool kids are calling sex now?"

"Yes."

"We will, Mom. We have your car... It's not like we need to boink in the old folks' home."

"How did I raise such a terrible child?"

"Just got lucky."

"I did. I think the world of you, child. I do hope you know that."

"And I couldn't have asked for a better mom. I hope you know that."

"Those how-to-be-a-cool-mom classes really paid off?"

"Yep."

"Good. Then it wasn't a waste of twenty dollars."

The detective laughed behind us. "You two are strange. Awesome but strange. Thanks for letting me into your little world of oddity."

"Our pleasure," I said, and meant it.

∞ ∞ ∞

"Where are we?" Fern had woken up after her after-dinner nap and stretched languidly in the passenger seat.

I tickled her side, mid-stretch, and relished in the sound of her squeal. "Somewhere in Ohio."

"I think I peed a little. That wasn't very nice. Rest area?"

I hadn't been paying any attention, so I wasn't sure. "I haven't seen one in a while, so hopefully one is coming up soon."

"Can we stop?"

"Of course. I could use a leg stretch."

"Thank you." She lay back in the seat again and put her shoeless feet up on the dash. Her shorts were riding up, and I took my hand off the shifter and slid them up and down her incredibly soft thighs.

"You're not helping."

"With what?"

"Me having to pee."

"Oh. Sorry."

"That's okay."

I still didn't stop, just smiled evilly instead. I owed her for the couch comments and tail flash.

"Dane." She squirmed in her seat.

"Yes?"

"I'm going to pee on the seat."

"Okay. I'll stop."

Ten minutes later, the first blue sign for a rest area appeared ahead. I pointed for Fern to see. "Five more minutes. Can you hold it?"

She nodded.

I'd hooked the car stereo to my phone, so I started my playlist. I'd shut it off while she was sleeping. Maybe some music would take her mind off her bladder.

Fern rolled her window down a little and stuck her fingers outside, testing the temperature. "It's getting colder."

"We probably won't see any snow. Still a bit early for that. Chicago usually sees its first around Thanksgiving. Sometimes."

"That's early."

"Well, it is cold as a well-digger's ass," I quoted my late, not-so-great father.

"Huh?"

"Nothing. Just something my father used to say."

"Do you miss him?"

"Yes. He was my father. Turned out to be kind of a douche the past year, but he loved me."

"Can I ask you something?"

"Always."

199

"I don't miss my mother. In fact, I'm kind of glad she's gone. Does that make me a horrible person?"

I opened my mouth to answer her but stopped myself. I thought about my words before I let them fly. "I think our love for our parents is proportional to the love and caring they gave us. Your mother had a set of problems I could only imagine dealing with. She saw what you were instead of who you were. She treated you horribly. I'm not going to lie. I saw your bedroom and your house. There was nothing of you there. No pictures, no art drawn in school, *nothing*. She was too focused on what had happened to her instead of what she was doing to you. So, to answer your question, no. It doesn't make you a horrible person. It makes you human."

She smiled at that, and I knew I had answered the question correctly. It paid to be honest. "Thank you," she said.

"For what?"

"Seeing who I am, rather than focusing on the what I am."

"Well, I can't help it. You are pretty awesome. It didn't hurt that you're as hot as you are." I gave her a little wink to let her know I was joking.

We pulled off at the rest stop, and I found a spot relatively close to the entrance. Unfortunately, it was one of those stops that just had bathrooms and vending machines. We had just had dinner a while ago, but I could use some snacks to help keep me going. Stale vended donuts didn't exactly sound that appetizing. I would, however, grab a Coke.

The lights flickered over our car. I half expected a horde of zombies to crest the hill behind the building. Why were there fewer things as creepy as a rest area at night? "Ready?" I asked her before popping open my door.

"Yep."

I got out and waited for her in front of the car. She practically ran past me in her need to pee, laughing as she headed for the door. Shaking my head, I sprinted in after her. I really didn't have to go, but I'd try. We would make more time on an empty tank.

The lobby was empty, and Fern had already gone into the women's side. I walked into the empty men's room and did my business, waiting for her out in the lobby.

I was standing by the front door when a big Harley pulled up into the spot next to where I had parked. The biker took off his half-helmet and set it on the seat, nearly charging for the door. I guessed Fern wasn't the only one with a squirrel bladder. In an effort to be gentlemanly, I opened the door for him as he ambled by.

"Thanks, kid," he called over his shoulder, and disappeared into the men's room.

Fern came out with a relieved look on her face.

"Feel better?"

She nodded.

"Want something to drink?"

"Do they have coffee?"

"I think you can call it that."

We headed toward the vending machines. I pulled out my wallet and found a five. I stuck it in the coffee machine, and after deciphering the secret code for extra-strength hot black coffee, I punched it in on the illuminated buttons. Fern squealed when the cup dropped into the holster and began filling. "Never seen one before?"

"No. That's cool."

"Yeah, well. You might not think so after you taste it. Mom always complained about rest area coffee. I'm going to grab a Coke."

I stepped two machines over and dropped in the dollar coins the coffee machine had given me back as change. At least with Coke, I only had one big button to press.

The door to the vending room opened and two guys in their thirties walked in. They ignored me and focused on the bent over Fern, who watched her brewing coffee.

"Hey, baby," one of them said, and caressed her ass as he walked by. "Why don't you let me buy you a real drink?"

I wanted to jump to her rescue but swallowed my pride. I'd just get in her way. Fern didn't need me to protect her. Not even a little bit. Instead, I unscrewed the cap to my Coke, leaned against the machine, and took a swallow, waiting for the show to start.

She stood up slowly, taking her hands off her knees and turning. "*You* do not get to touch me there. Ever. Only *he* is allowed to touch my butt." She pointed to me.

I raised my Coke in salute.

"What, you think his little bitch ass is going to protect you?"

She blinked at him in confusion. "There are only two of you. Why would I need his help?"

The other one laughed. "You think you can take the both of us?"

She nodded in confusion again. He turned to me and pointed at Fern.

"Twenty bucks says you won't last ten seconds," I said.

"This is bullshit," the ass grabber said, and clasped her wrist. "Why don't we get that drink?"

"Don't kill them," I warned.

"What if it's an accident?"

"I'm sure you can claim self-defense, but if you get blood in my mother's car, she's going to be mad at you."

"Do your grandparents not have cleaning supplies?"

"Yeah, but blood is tricky. Sometimes it stains, and the floorboards are gray. I argued for a darker color, but you know Mom can be stubborn. She treats me like a kid sometimes and doesn't listen."

"Are you two fricking kidding me right now?" Ass Grabber was getting angrier. That had been my intention. I wanted him to have a *small* chance.

Fern rolled her eyes. "You're very rude." She slowly lifted her arm, the one he was holding. He grinned at her and pushed against it, slowly realizing the gravity of the situation as he couldn't stop her or even slow down her movement.

"Grab her, Dave."

"Are you kidding me?" He took a step closer. Fern's other hand shot out and backhanded him. His head snapped back, and his eyes rolled up, a huge red welt instantaneously appearing on his forehead. He dropped and groaned, clutching his face.

"What the hell are you?"

She pulled him closer, and he let go of her wrist. She grabbed his jacket, preventing him from running. Her horns curled out of her head, and her eyes glowed red, flames dancing behind them.

He screamed as she lifted him and slammed him into the wall. She snarled and snapped at the exposed flesh of his stomach, not tearing into him as I would have expected with the elongated fangs she hadn't showed me before. She didn't want to hurt him, just scare him. Her little display had its intended effect. A very large wet stain appeared on the front of his pants and quickly spread down the entire leg before dripping down on the floor. She stopped and gave him a disgusted frown before dropping him. He sat there staring at her and shaking uncontrollably.

She sucked in a breath of air and shook her head, her fangs and everything else returning to normal. "Never touch a lady without asking."

The guy nodded. She kicked him in the face, and he was out like a light. I began clapping, and she gave me a little bow, grinning with pride.

I motioned to the door, seeing the biker was standing on the other side of it. He opened it and made a sweeping gesture for us to exit first, smiling as we passed.

"Sorry about the mess," I said, vainly hoping he hadn't witnessed the whole show.

"No worries, kid. Have a safe trip."

"Thanks."

"Oh, and don't worry. I didn't see anything," he said with a wink of a glowing red eye.

I chuckled nervously and nodded.

CHAPTER 23

It was almost one in the morning by the time we pulled into the grandparents' driveway. "We made it," I said to myself, as Fern was passed out in the front seat beside me.

I shut off the car and reached over, gently shaking her leg. "What?" She sat up and groggily rubbed her eyes.

"We're here. Come on."

She nodded and undid her seatbelt, pulling the lever and raising her seat up. We got out, and I hit the button on the key fob to open the trunk. My suitcase tumbled free and Fern's hand shot out, catching it by the handle before it hit the ground.

"Nice reflexes."

"Thanks."

I took my bag from her and grabbed the giant bag of laundry we had packed up, leaving her floral print suitcase for her to bring in. Closing the trunk, I hit the lock button, and we headed toward my grandparents' front porch. There was a note on the front door.

I yanked it down and held it up to the light over our heads.

Your grandfather is old. We're going to bed. Leftovers in the fridge if you're hungry. Made up the spare room for the two of you.

Gramma She even drew an emoji on the note.

I laughed. Not at Gramma's signature, but at the winky face she had drawn at the end of her note.

"Guess we're bunking together," I said to Fern, who had just finished reading the note.

"I like your Gramma already."

I opened the unlocked front door, brought our stuff in, locking up behind us. I'd yell at Gramma in the morning for leaving it unlocked, even if it was for a good cause.

"I'm going to take our stuff to our room, if you want to pick through the fridge."

"I'll help, and then we can look together."

"I like this plan," I said, and gave her a kiss before hoisting the suitcase and garbage bag up off the floor. We made our way up the ancient wooden staircase, and I pointed in the direction of the guest room.

I set the suitcase on the dresser and set the bag on the floor, grabbing Fern's stuff and placing it next to mine. We could unpack in the morning.

Fern fell backward on the bed and started making comforter angels in its fluffy softness. "This is huge. The biggest bed I've ever been in."

I had a tendency to forget that there were many things Fern had never experienced. The coffee vending machine was a good example. She'd lived sheltered her whole life, limited to school and the town of Oak Hills. As far as I knew, she had never ventured past city limits. Her home life hadn't exactly been a mecca of worldly experiences either. Her room had looked more like a jail cell than a teenage girl's room.

"Yeah. It's a king. Mine is only a double, and the air mattress is a twin. There's a bigger bed called a California king, too," I explained patiently.

Her eyes got big. "Woah. Can we get one someday?"

"Does that mean you want to marry me?" I winked, letting her know I was joking.

She blushed and nodded.

My heart melted. At least I wouldn't be as nervous when I finally *did* propose. Properly. With a ring and a fancy dinner. Sometime well after college, and when we had stable jobs, and our own house.

"Come on. Let's go get some of Gramma's leftovers."

We headed downstairs just in time to see Grampa's ass sticking out of the fridge, while he rummaged.

"Hey, Grampa."

He shot up and spun around in his flannel bathrobe. "Don't tell Gramma I was grazing."

"Secret's safe," I said, and walked over, giving him a big hug. "Grampa, this is my girlfriend, Fern. Fern, this is Grampa."

"Pleased to meet you," she said, and held out her hand, which he used to pull her into his big, meaty arms. She smiled at me and rested her head on his chest.

"Welcome to the family, little lady. Take care of this brat for me, okay?"

Fern nodded as he let go of her. The light flicked on, and Gramma squealed, running across the kitchen to hug us both at the same time.

I introduced the ladies and pushed Grampa out of the way to get at the food. The three of them were sitting around chatting while I heated up two plates of barbequed chicken, egg noodles, and buttered corn.

I set Fern's in front of her with a fork and a Coke. She ate and talked while mine heated, answering their questions mostly truthfully and smiling every time she popped a bite of food into her mouth. My grandmother's cooking was like that. Simple, delicious, and it warmed the cockles of your heart.

She was only halfway done with her food when I sat down, a first for her. She ate faster than a garbage disposal most of the time. It took a lot of fuel to be that sexy.

"So, how's school?" Gramma asked, and then giggled. "Never mind. Not so hot, I guess."

"It's actually not as bad as you think, aside from the murders. Stood up to the football team, and made a bunch of friends. And met the girl of my dreams," I added with a smile at Fern.

"That was so sweet, I might just hurl," Grampa said with a chuckle. "Smooth talker, you are. Just like your father."

I nodded, not sure if that was a compliment or not.

"The day he asked for your mother's hand in marriage, I was all prepared to tell him to go packing. He was so slick, he not only got me to agree, but got us to let them live here for the first year of marriage! Smooth talker that one. I wasn't shocked when he became a lawyer. I'm sorry for your loss."

"Thanks, Grampa."

"So, what are you kids up to tomorrow?"

"I was thinking about taking Fern downtown. Take her for some real pizza and hot dogs. See the Willis Tower and the Hancock."

"You mean the Sears Tower."

"They renamed it, Grampa."

"I know they did. But it will always be the Sears Tower. Be strong, Dane."

I laughed. "I kind of like calling it Willis Tower. Makes me think of Nakatomi Plaza."

"You guys should come for Christmas break. We can do the Miracle Mile and see the lights. Then, we can watch Die Hard, the greatest Christmas movie ever made."

"Can we?" Fern asked shyly.

"If you want."

She nodded vigorously as she pushed her empty plate forward a little. It looked like she had licked it clean. There wasn't even any barbecue sauce on the plate. Just a couple of chicken bones. Judging by Gramma's face, she actually might have licked it.

"Well, we're going to bed," Gramma said, leaving little room for Grampa to argue. "There's pie in the fridge if you're still hungry." She touched Fern's shoulder as she said it. "You kids have a good sleep, and we'll see you in the morning. I'll make breakfast. Grampa made beef sausage."

"What's beef sausage?"

"An ancient family tradition passed down from the earliest German settlers of the region. It's actually called winterwurst." I even said it with Vs instead of Ws. "It's slow cooked beef and spices ground up with oats and onions. You slice it and fry it until it's crispy and put it on Wonder Bread. Not any fancy bread. Gotta use the Wonder stuff to get the correct taste and texture," I said reverently. I hadn't had any in a year. I was Jonesin'.

Grampa laughed. "Spoken like a true Wolf."

"Who's a wolf?"

"Dane. Wolf is our last name." He pointed at Gramma and himself.

"Oh," she said, impressed.

"Night, kids," Gramma said again, and tugged the sleeve of Grampa's robe.

"Night," I called softly as they headed to their room in the back of the house on the first floor. I figured that was the only reason they still had the house. If their bedroom were on the second, and they had to deal with stairs every night, they would have sold it and moved to Florida long ago.

I grabbed the plates, scraped them, and stuck them in the dishwasher. "Want some pie?"

"What kind?"

"I don't know. It will be good, either way." I opened the fridge and dug through the contents until I saw the pie, covered in tin foil. Grabbing it, the can of whip cream, and the milk, I set everything on the counter. It was cherry. I put the whip cream back and grabbed the ice cream out of the freezer instead.

I cut two slices and popped them in the microwave together. When they were warm, I took them out and plopped a schlarf of vanilla on top of them and grabbed two spoons. Setting the pie on the table, I got us the required glass of milk and sat back down.

Fern poked at it nervously.

"Never had cherry pie?"

"Not like this."

"Try it. Get a bit of ice cream with each bite, or you'll ruin it."

She nodded and did as I recommended. Her eyes closed as she rolled the experience around on her tongue and moaned.

"Yep. Nothing quite like Gramma's cherry pie. I don't know how she gets the sugar to stay on the crust like that. Every time Mom tries it, it turns brown."

"This is *good*. Like, yeah. Wow."

"Glad we came?"

"You don't know. I… I like being part of your family." She started crying, blinking as she ate. I reached over and rubbed her cheek. She pressed her face against my hand.

"I like you being part of my family." I kissed her. The chilly ice cream and the cherries flavored the kiss perfectly. She pushed the pie away and slid her chair in front of me, not stopping the kiss. Her hands found their way to my chest. I pulled away, panting. "We are not making out in my grandparents' kitchen." I smiled, promising her a continuation elsewhere.

"Sorry, but that tasted better than the pie."

"Yes. You do."

She squirmed in her seat as she hurried and ate the rest *very* quickly.

I chuckled and finished mine off in record time, too.

210

She started pulling on me. "Let me put everything away and clean up quick. You think Mom's scary? Leave Gramma's kitchen dirty. Land wars in Asia have started for less."

She harrumphed and sat back down.

I rinsed the cherry goop of the plates and forks, slid them in the dishwasher and put the pie and everything else away, and wiped off the counter.

"Ready for bed?"

She nearly growled.

I laughed and held out my hand. My feet might have touched three or four of the steps as she dragged me up the flight and practically threw me into the bed.

"Second desserts?"

She shut the door and lifted her hoodie and shirt off her in one fluid motion, her wings spreading behind her. Stepping out of her leggings, she left her panties on but pulled them down, letting her tail fly free. She was hotter than the sexiest girl I could imagine. I unbuckled my jeans, slid them down over my boxers and kicked them off before she tore them from my flesh.

She growled low in the back of her throat, her horns protruding from her forehead.

"No teeth or nails!" I managed to get the words out before she pounced on me, landing on my waist. She kissed me as she backed herself into my lap. I could still taste the cherries and cream as she took my breath away. For the first time, we made love with the lights on. The beauty of it would be burned into my brain forever.

When we finished, we lay under the heavy down comforter, and spooned. It felt even better. I absolutely loved the demon in my arms. I was hooked, trapped, and hopelessly addicted, the happiest guy in the world.

"Just thought of something. What am I going to call you when we get married? You won't be Fern anymore, you'll be Evans."

She sighed happily. "Yours."

"Huh?"

"You can call me yours."

A tear wet my cheek. Then, I knew the difference between happy and euphoric.

CHAPTER 24

We stepped on the train, and Fern glanced around nervously, sniffing the air. "This is safe?"

"More than driving downtown."

She nodded, and we found a couple of empty seats next to each other. The morning rush had already passed through and the train, while not deserted, wasn't as packed as it could have been.

"I told the grandparents we would be out late and spend the day with them tomorrow. So, sky is the limit today. Wherever you want to go, whatever you want to do. If you see something, let me know."

"Okay."

She watched the changing scenery through the dingey window of the train and gasped when the city proper started whizzing by. I reached over and gently shut her mouth when the skyscrapers in the horizon came into view.

"Impressive, isn't it?"

All she could do was nod.

"See that *really* tall one?"

"Yes?"

"We're going to the top of that. The observation deck. You can stand in glass balconies that tilt out over the city street. Sound like fun?"

"No. What if we fall?"

"Well, one of us has wings…"

"But I can't fly. They're too small."

"I bet you can glide like hell, though," I said with a wink.

"Maybe. I never tried."

"Well, hopefully you won't have to today."

We got off and wandered through the city. We hopped on a bus and went to Navy Pier. We had lunch. We laughed. Mid-afternoon, I bought her a piece of cheesecake at the base of the Hancock and took her up to observation deck. While not as tall as the Willis Tower, it was still pretty damn impressive. Fern gasped as we looked down at the tiny people below, scurrying like ants.

She wrapped her arms around me after that, grinning from ear to ear. "Thank you."

"The date isn't over, yet."

We walked lazily through Water Tower Place, bought candy, and held hands. And then, just as the sun started to sink, we made our way to the Willis Tower and rode the express elevator to the observation deck. I had to hold her hand to get her to gingerly walk out onto the glass. "It's safe, I promise."

She took one last large step and settled next to me, gripping me around my stomach.

"See that over there?"

She looked up.

"That's Wisconsin."

"What's a Wisconsin?"

"The state? Green Bay. Cheese?"

"I know, Dane. I was joking."

"Oh."

She giggled into my jacket.

We sat there as the sun finally went down, the city lighting up and pushing the darkness back. She smiled at the beauty of it all. "I think we should move here one day."

"I don't think you can live here."

"I meant Chicago."

"I know. It was my turn to make a joke."

"You need to work on those."

I laughed and kissed her head.

"So, you want to live in Chicago with a king-sized bed. Anything else?"

"A dog named Kitty and a cat named Puppy."

That made me laugh. "Why?"

"Cuz it's funny."

"Deal. Anything else? What about children?"

She got that panicky look in her eyes as she backed up onto solid ground again, shaking her head.

"You don' t want a child?"

"No. Do you?"

"Maybe one day." I walked over to her and grabbed her hands. "Do you mind if I ask why?"

"What if I had one and resented it? What if I hated it? I don't want to do to my child what my mother did to me."

I pulled her into a hug. "That tells me right now that you never would. You love me and always express that, why would you worry about your child?"

"I don't know. I'm just afraid."

"Well, we have years and years to think about it. I'm not in a rush, though we should probably be very careful…"

"No. Succubae are…a little different. The detective told me when he taught me what I was. Can't get pregnant unless we want to."

"Well, that's convenient."

She nodded and grinned. "So, you don't have to worry about that."

"Wish you had told me sooner…" I laughed.

"I'm telling you now." She looked at me, her eyes flaring with heat, and gently kissed me.

"Yeah. Don't you start, missy. You wait until we get home to start giving me those looks." I winked and kissed her nose, not having any desire to get arrested by the CPD for getting frisky in the Willis Tower.

She pouted.

I kissed her lip. "No."

She laughed and let go. "We should probably get home, then."

"Now that's a damn good idea. We can grab some hot dogs on the way. Are you hungry?"

"I'm always hungry. But a wiener does sound...delicious."

"Oh, my God. What are you some kind of–"

"Succubus?"

I nodded, smiling.

"Yep."

"Lucky me."

∞ ∞ ∞

We made it to the train station by my grandparents' house and started the walk back. It wasn't even nine at night. I hoped they were still up. I would have liked to say goodnight to them before bed. I was also looking forward to a hot shower. It wasn't hot out, but walking all over the city had taken its toll on me, and my deodorant had run out of viability before dinner.

"I stink," I told Fern as we walked out onto the sidewalk and headed north. "I *really* want a shower."

She leaned in and sniffed me. "You smell good."

"No way. I'm ripe."

"Seriously. I like the way you smell. Even now."

"You must be in love."

"I am."

I leaned over and smelled her. She still smelled good. Maybe half-demons didn't even need deodorant. "You cheat."

"How?"

"You smell like you always do. Like my body wash and strawberries."

"I smell fruity?"

"Yep."

"Huh."

We laughed, and she bumped my hip with hers. We were a few hundred feet from my grandparents when she froze and stared in the direction of their house, her face twisting in anger.

"What?"

"He's here."

"Who?" I asked, even though I didn't need to. As soon as the question left my mouth, I knew the answer and started running toward my grandparents.

Fern passed me, only slowing once she hit the porch. She stopped and stared. When I caught up, I saw at what. My grandfather, bleeding from a wound on his head on the floor of the living room. My grandmother was nowhere in sight. Someone had kicked in the door, and it hung from the top hinge, swinging in the evening breeze. I lurched forward and fell to the floor by Grampa's still form.

"Please don't be dead, please don't be dead," I chanted as I checked his pulse. I didn't need to. His chest rose and fell rhythmically. He was breathing. Fern handed me one of the decorative pillows off the couch, then raced toward the kitchen.

I lifted his head, sticking the pillow under it as fast as I could, and lurched toward the direction she had gone. I might not be of any help, but I sure as hell wasn't going to let her do it alone.

My grandmother was in a chair in the center of the kitchen. He must have found my grampa's stash of zip-ties he kept in the junk drawer. He had bound her hands and feet to the wooden seat. Someone had taped a note with an address to her chest with the words, *Come alone, Lucy*, scrawled neatly beneath it.

Fern grabbed the note.

I snagged the kitchen shears and cut Gramma loose, gently pulling the tape from her mouth. "Are you okay?"

"Yes! Your grandfather!"

"He's unconscious, but alive. In the living room. I'm sorry, Gramma."

"This was all that sick bastard. You couldn't know he'd follow you." She kissed my cheek before running to check on Grampa. I followed her to the door to make sure she got there okay.

I blinked at my grandmother. For the first time, someone had seen who was behind all of it. We knew it was Fern's father, but his identity was still a mystery.

"Call an ambulance, call the detective, and call your mother," Fern said, leaving no room for argument.

"Fern, you can't go."

"He knows where your grandparents *live*, Dane. You want him to come back?"

"Who cares? We'll take them and leave. You can't go."

"I have to, Dane. Or this will never end."

"Please." I did the only thing I could do, I begged. "I can't live without you."

"Yes, you can. But I'm not planning on going with him or dying. We don't even know what he wants."

"Okay. But screw that. I'm going with you."

"Trust me, Dane. You don't want to. If this comes down to a fight… even I don't stand a chance."

"Then we'll just have to be smart about it. Give me five minutes to talk to Gramma and make some calls."

"You're sure?"

"Never been more sure about anything in my life. I'd rather die with you than live without you. Can you understand that?"

"Oh. I do. I know exactly what you mean."
"Then we do this together?"
She nodded.

CHAPTER 25

I pulled the SUV into the parking lot of a hotel. The address matched the note. I wiped my sweaty palms on my jeans, taking deep, slow breaths to avoid hyperventilating.

"Great. We're here, but how the hell are we supposed to find him?"

"Same way I knew he was at your grandparents. I can feel him."

"Lead the way."

We got out of the car and headed toward the lobby. If he was a guest at the hotel, we wouldn't even know what name to ask for. We didn't have to. We both recognized the man standing in the parking lot waiting for us.

"Dean Winchester?" I stopped in my tracks, looking from him to Fern and back again. Repeatedly. I didn't want to believe it, but it made *so* much sense. How he always looked out for Lucy, letting her off the hook, shadowing her every movement.

"Hello, Dane. Hello, daughter. I thought I made it clear that you were to come alone?"

"You know me. Disobedient as all hell. How did you know we were in Chicago?" Fern didn't seem that shocked. If I had found out the dean of my high school was *my* biological father, I'd probably be needing some therapy. Hell, I might need some anyway.

He turned to me. "You may thank your mother for calling the school to let us know you would not be attending. She even gave us your grandparents' names and number should we need to contact you." He grinned wickedly, pleased with how easy we had made it for him.

I groaned inwardly. We set up the perfect scenario for him, but there was still so much I didn't understand. "Why? What do you want? Why did you follow us here?"

He stepped forward. "It's very simple. You see, Lucy turned eighteen today."

I looked at her. "It's your birthday?"

"What's the date?" She blinked at me, totally unaware.

"The twenty-ninth..."

"Yes. I guess so?"

"So, what does her turning eighteen have to do with it?" I turned to him for the answers I'd never get from Fern.

He took a step closer, looking at Fern and trying to see something that I couldn't. "You can feel it, can't you, daughter?"

It was almost as if she didn't *want* to answer. I could see the word forming on her lips, and her jaw clenching to keep it from escaping. "Yes," she hissed through grinding teeth.

"What?" As much as she didn't want to give him an answer, I had a feeling I wanted to hear the answer even less.

She gave me a confused stare, unsure herself.

"She's come into her full power. Once I get her away from you, her silly bonded human, she will be mine!" He licked his lips greedily.

And then it clicked. Why he had gone out of his way to protect me, too. I was bonded with his daughter. If anything happened to me, it happened to her. My stomach twisted in a knot, disgust threatening to waste all of the food we had stuffed ourselves with. "You want your daughter?" This time, I *knew* I didn't want to hear the answer.

"No. I want her power. It is what I feed upon." He took another step forward, and his bones began to crack as he awkwardly tried to stay upright. Giant black wings burst from his back in a spray of blood and gore. His skin sloughed from his frame as he grew to twice his size, his skin darkening to the same color and texture as his wings. Giant fangs sprouted from his upper and lower jaw, and dagger-like talons sprang from the tips of his fingers. His feet elongated, and the balls raised off the ground as they took on an animalistic shape.

Fern had been right about one thing. I wanted to shit my pants.

The detective had been right about something else, also. Demons did feed on different things. Having a father that could feed off your power was the final short shit stick in the parental drawing. Her mother was insane, and her father was an evil bastard of a demon. *At least he didn't* want *her, want her.*

I pulled the samurai sword from where I'd hidden it in my jacket. Some grandfathers collected sports memorabilia, mine collected swords from all over the world. Lucky for me. It was thin and light enough to conceal. Hidden in my coat, the handle had been behind my head and the blade had been hanging down my back. If he had snuck up behind us, he would have seen it. I just hoped it was enough to give Fern an edge against his claws and teeth. The sword wasn't for me, it was for her.

"Fern!" I tossed it to her, and she caught it without even looking. My girlfriend was so badass.

The demon snarled as she flung the scabbard from the blade. It landed in the bushes next to her. Steel could cut the demon, something I learned from my discussion with the good detective before we drove to Chicago. I'd called him again before we drove to the meeting point and asked if he was sure steel would work. He promised me it would, along with a promise not to tell my mother what the hell was going on. He gave me a list of *everything* that could hurt and kill a demon. The list was short, and they were frigging hard to kill. Heart and head had to be removed. Even if we survived, this was going to get ugly.

Fern pulled off her hoodie and T-shirt, leaving just a tank top that let her wings be free. She snarled at her father, and her talons, tail, teeth, and horns sprang forth much like his had done. There was no slow painful growth. I saw what he meant about her powers. Even her wings seemed to grow, until the tips nearly touched the ground. She was deadly and beautiful. I just hoped she could beat the giant creature standing in front of her.

"You killed my mother, you asshole."

"You're welcome," he said through elongated teeth, drool falling to the ground below him. He hissed with evil laughter, curling his talons upward.

She screamed and charged, the blade sparking off his talons as he easily blocked the strike I could hardly see. That was her job, keep him distracted and fighting. And don't get hit.

My job was much easier. I pulled my jacket off and grabbed the pump shotgun out of the open window of the car while Fern kept him busy. Once Grampa had woken up, we'd told him what we needed. A sword for Fern, and something else for me. I'd remembered the tale my mother had told me about my father's serenade...

I pumped the shotgun, the shell full of rock salt slammed into place as I circled behind their intense fight. The demon wasn't even paying attention to the lowly human. I stepped a little closer, not wanting to hit Fern with the spray I was about to unload. I checked the safety, just like Grampa showed me, and sighted down the barrel, aiming right between the wings. I ducked, narrowly dodging his swishing tail, sighted again, and pulled the trigger.

The shotgun didn't have a stock to brace against my shoulder, and the blast nearly knocked half my teeth out. But the effect was glorious.

The demon screamed and arched its back as the large chunks of rock salt sizzled in its skin. It was a minor irritation at most, not having the penetrating power of slugs or shot, but it did the trick. It spun in anger and bore down on me with every intention of smearing me across the asphalt.

I had just enough time to pump the shotgun one last time as I aimed at his head and pulled the trigger. Winchester blocked the blast with his arm, catching the salt in the soft part of its flesh. The skin sizzled again, and the arm fell to his side. The pain was enough of a distraction for me to pump another round into the chamber. The demon lifted his good arm high above his head to smash me into the pavement...and Fern struck with the sword, a swiping arc right in the back of the neck.

Again, he screamed in agony, covering the wound, leaving his front wide open for another shotgun blast...

I'll admit it. It wasn't my proudest moment. I shot from the hip right where I'd been aiming. Right in his demon junk.

The arm dropped from the wound on his neck and covered the salt-peppered wound at the apex of his thighs as he wailed in misery.

"No more kids for you."

I chambered another and pulled the trigger, catching him right in the face. Shot after shot exploded from the shotgun. His face began smoking and caught on fire in several places. Then a primal scream tore through the night as Fern attacked from the air, the sword cleanly cleaving through the demon's neck.

Winchester's head rolled forward, stopping just short of my feet, staring lifelessly up into the sky. We'd done it. Once we took his heart from his chest, the nightmare would be over.

I remembered the old adage, "Never count your chickens before they hatch." I don't know why it crossed my mind until the headless body lurched forward and swiped me with five six-inch-long talons. Pain seared my chest as I flew through the air. Then blackness.

CHAPTER 26

I woke up in my grandparents' spare bedroom, my chest on fire. Every attempt to breathe hurt like someone had stuffed my lungs with hedgehogs.

"Ow," I wheezed.

Fern was lying on the bed next to me. She blinked and sat up, a worried frown on her face.

"What happened?" I wanted to sit up, but couldn't find the energy.

Her face crumpled, and she began sobbing, dropping her head to my lap. My mother and Brian came rushing into the room, my grandparents behind them. They all gathered around the bed, worry straining their faces.

"What?"

"How are you feeling, kid?" Brian sat on the edge of the bed, running his fingers over my face.

"I'm guessing I'm pretty messed up?"

"You died three times."

"Why am I still here?"

He nodded at Fern. "She kept healing you."

"How?"

"How do you think a succubus heals someone? Hmmm?"

"Oh. *Oh!* That's how I healed from the beer bottle isn't it?"

He nodded.

"I still think we should have taken him to a hospital," Mom said indignantly.

"Ew. You didn't watch?"

"What? No!" She turned seven shades of red and shut up.

Gramma just giggled at her.

"I still hurt. Is it going to go away?"

"More healing, and you'll be good as new. You poor thing," the detective said with a chuckle. That earned him a slap on the arm from Mom.

"So, you all know everything now?"

"Yes. Brian filled us all in. I still can't believe you two fought that thing."

"I just want to know how we got away with it. I was blasting that damn thing with the shotgun, and not a single cop showed up. Granted... this is Chicago, but still."

"You didn't feel the spell?" Fern lifted her head from my lap.

"What spell?"

"Magic. My father cast a shield as soon as we saw him. It collapsed as soon as I cut his heart from his chest and put the blade through it."

"You did?"

She nodded.

"You were amazing, by the way."

"You both were," Brian chimed in. "A changed demon, taken down by a seventeen-year-old human and a half-demon. I've never heard of such a thing, not in all my six-hundred years."

"So, you told Mom about you, too."

"Yep. No secrets."

"You're okay with that?" I looked up at her, and she nodded slowly.

"Took some getting used to, but I love Fern as if she were my own. I should have no problem loving another demon. I just told him never to change in front of me."

"Good call. I almost shit my pants."

Brian chuckled.

"So, what else did I miss?"

"After it was dead, it evaporated into smoke. I grabbed you and brought you back here and began to heal you."

"Gramma and I sat downstairs and listened to the radio very loudly, Dane."

I laughed at Grampa, arms crossing my chest as pain lanced through my entire body from the strain. "How you feeling? How's your head?" I tilted my head, trying to get a better look at his.

"I'm fine. Just grateful that thing didn't hurt your grandmother."

"I'm just glad all of that is over."

"Me, too," Fern chimed in, and wrapped her arms around my waist.

"Looks like it's time for another healing. You kids have fun," Brian said, and started motioning for everyone to leave the room.

Mom stuck her fingers in her ears and started chanting, "La la la la la la."

I chucked as the door clicked shut.

"Thanks, Fern."

"For what?"

"Keeping me alive and being the best damn girlfiend a guy could hope for."

"Thanks for staying alive. Silly human," she said, and kissed me before healing the last of my wounds.

Epilogue

The tux squeezed my shoulders too tightly, making the simple act of raising my arms impossible, but Mom insisted it looked fantastic. I think she was even happier than I was.

I stood next to Brian. After five years, he and I had grown a lot closer. He stepped up and really became the head of our family. He'd even proposed to my mother two years after they started dating. It had gotten to the point where I couldn't imagine our lives without him, and it saddened me to think how lonely he would be when we were all but a fond memory in his mind. That closeness we had developed was why I asked him to be my best man.

I looked behind me to the guests, all seated in white wooden folding chairs wrapped in more flowers than I had ever seen in my entire life. I waved at Gramma in the front row. She and Grampa had flown out to Oak Hills for Fern's and my graduation from the University of Virginia and our wedding. They looked so proud yesterday as we both received our degrees. I still couldn't believe I had graduated with honors. After the honeymoon, I would be heading to Quantico for training to become an FBI agent. Apparently, Brian had more than a few friends in the FBI. Fern was using the money she got from the settlement with the psychiatric hospital to open a Japanese cuisine restaurant downtown. Hell Bento. I thought it was catchy, but tried to talk her out of it.

The string quartet began playing the Pachelbel Cannon as the bridesmaids started down the aisle with the groomsmen. We each had only picked three. I nodded at Valerie in the lead. When we had returned to school, she and Fern had a huge knock down brawl. They brawled, and Fern knocked her down. After that, they became really good friends, Valerie having earned a new respect for the once quiet, hoodie-wearing, purple-haired girl. Once she could make her wings go away, that all changed. She let her hair grow out into its natural white, and she looked even more stunning, yet elegant, by the time we graduated high school. Valerie was even going to be the manager of the restaurant. She walked with James. One of my friends from college.

My other two groomsmen were two of the football players from high school. Once we had gotten back, they sort of adopted me by way of apology. We found out we had more in common than we thought, the two of them being geekier than they were willing to let on. We went to many parties together. Fern's other bride's maids were my groomsmen's girlfriends. Funny how the world works.

Her matron of honor, however, was none other than my mother. She strode alone down the aisle, seven months pregnant. And smiling lovingly at the demon standing next to me at the altar. And here, she'd been cautioning me the whole time. Apparently, only female demons could control their pregnancies. Male demons, not so much. The baby hadn't been planned, but they were both ecstatic. It was a girl, of course. They had already seen the wings in the ultrasound. Mom had an OBGYN who was a demon friend of Brian's sister. Brian's sister was also helping Fern with the intricacies of opening a restaurant. They had become quite close, too.

I smiled in satisfaction at how my life turned out. It never ceased to amaze me sometimes. I thought I couldn't be happier… Until the quartet stopped the music and began strumming the opening bars to the bridal march.

I held my breath and waited for Fern to come into view. Finally, she came out through the flowered arch and my heart began beating faster than it had ever beat before. Her dress was made of a gossamer film over a shining fabric wrapped tightly around her body and flowing freely behind her, carried by three of the children of her various friends, dressed all in white. She looked like she had stepped from the pages of a fairy tale. One written for me. She was my queen, my princess, and my reason for living. I couldn't wait to say "I do."

Grampa had the honor of walking her down the aisle, proud as the proverbial peacock. He marched her right up to me, grabbed my arm, and put her hand on mine. "Don't screw this up, kiddo."

"I won't, Grampa."

He smiled and nodded, moving back a little.

"Greetings. Who gives the bride to this man today?"

"I do." Grampa smiled at the Justice of the Peace.

"And you are?"

"Her grandfather."

Fern sucked in a breath, and I could almost hear the tear that fell down her cheek.

"Then let us begin."

I took her hand from my arm, and then lifted the light veil from her face, letting it fall behind her.

"We are gathered here today to witness this man, Dane Evans, join together with this woman, Lucy Fern, in the bonds of matrimony."

I couldn't take my eyes off my bride, and the justice's words floated around me like the notes of music wafting from the quartet. All I could hear was the beating of my heart and the beating of Fern's and another, light and fluttery, in the background. Fern's eyes met mine and my world exploded in light. She smiled. She had something she wanted to tell me, and she couldn't wait.

I cocked my eyebrow at her and returned her smile.

I must have zoned out for a moment because before I knew it, the time to say my vows had come.

"I, Dane Evans, promise to be your husband from this time forward, and for all times after that. I promise to love you, cherish you, and always be by your side. I promise to help you when you need me, be patient when you don't, and love you every moment in between."

Brian handed me a band of white gold etched with a pair of wings, and I slipped it on her finger.

"I, Lucy Evans, promise to be your wife from this time forward, and for all times after that. I promise to love you, cherish you, and always be by your side. I promise to be a good mother to your child and love her with all my heart, teaching her the meaning of the word love and all that comes with it. I promise to love her as much as I love you as we spend the rest of our lives together as a family, as you and yours have taught me."

My mouth dropped open as Fern proudly rubbed her tiny belly. Her vows had completely deviated from what she had practiced at the rehearsal and what I had seen her write. A collective gasp rose from the crowd as she proudly told me we were going to have a baby.

She reached over and put a band of black gold on my finger, etched with silver wings.

"You may now kiss the bride, the mother to be," the justice said happily.

My ears roared from the collective cheer that erupted behind us. I could feel it reverberating through my chest as my lips met hers. The sound of my blood pulsing through my ears as Fern poured every ounce of love into that kiss completely drowned out the cacophony of everything around us, and it was just us.

"I love you, my wife," I whispered as I pulled away.
"I love you, too, my husband."

About the Author

A late comer to the writing game, Jacquelyn had always been a fan of romance novels and lately become addicted to the reverse harem category. I mean seriously, who wouldn't? Sitting alone one night she flipped open her laptop and said, "I'm going to give this a whirl." And thus, the Lovin' the Coven series was given life. She has designs on other series as well, but only time shall tell.

As for her, she is five-foot-something, with graying hair, wicked eyes, an eager smile, and an annoying laugh. She lives at home with her dog, a cat, and that is about all she is comfortable sharing.